"Let me present, the lovely Can—dy!"

Taking her cue, Eryn surged up, flipping the top layer of the cake back and standing tall. For one satisfying moment, Eryn spotted Callan on the other side of the room. The big man stood near the balcony doors, totally fixated on her. At that moment, the suite's door crashed inward and a group of men wearing ski masks invaded the room. They carried pistols and small machine guns. A masked man grabbed one of the guys at the party and put a pistol to his head. Another masked man fired a burst that punched out glass from the balcony doors.

"Get down on the floor! Do it now and you'll live!"

D0711308

★ ★ ★

Dear Reader,

The idea for this story came to me in a dream. The mercenary heartthrob looking out for his baby sister is a definite winner for me. *An Officer and a Gentleman* still gets me. Callan Storm hasn't had the benefit of that pristine life in the military, though. He's a behind-the-scenes operator, a member of a Black Ops group, and he doesn't trust much. I do love those rugged guys who will see a promise through to the end no matter what risks they take.

I wanted to give Callan someone he could trust— eventually. But I didn't want her to appear totally together and at her best because then the professional side of my school of hard knocks soldier might recognize a kindred spirit. So I stashed security specialist Eryn McAdams inside a cake at a bachelor's party. And I made her a last-minute change in the lineup. I thought, Callan will never trust anyone like that when something goes wrong. I was right! Join them for the night of their lives when everything changes—at the speed of a bullet.

Happy reading!

Meredith Fletcher

MEREDITH FLETCHER

Best Man for the Job

ROMANTIC
SUSPENSE

Recycling programs
for this product may
not exist in your area.

ISBN-13: 978-0-373-27740-7

BEST MAN FOR THE JOB

www.Harlequin.com

Printed in U.S.A.

Books by Meredith Fletcher

Harlequin Romantic Suspense
Best Man for the Job #1670

Silhouette Bombshell
Dead-Ringer #14
Look-Alike #90
Storm Watcher #120

Athena Force
Vendetta
Beneath the Surface

Silhouette Single Title
Femme Fatale
"The Get-Away Girl"

MEREDITH FLETCHER

lives out west where the skies are big, but still close
enough to Los Angeles to slip in for some strategic
shopping. She loves old stores with real wooden floors,
open-air cafés, comfortable boots, the mountains and
old movies like *Portrait of Jennie* while sipping a cup of
hot cocoa on a frosty day. She's previously written for
Silhouette Bombshell and loves action romances with
larger-than-life heroes and heroines with pithy repartee.
She has pithy repartee herself, but never when she
seems to need it most! She's much more comfortable
at the computer writing her books. Please contact
her at meredithfletcher@hotmail.com or find her at
www.whatmakesmyheartbeatfaster.blogspot.com.

For Montana, a great little mother.
And for Mary-Theresa Hussey,
for all the laughs and guidance.

Chapter 1

"You're not the girl I was expecting."

Choking down the immediate surge of irritation that raced through her, Eryn McAdams studied the tall man blocking her path into the hotel suite. She'd just come from a day filled with dealing with macho security types treating her like a "girl." She was only here now as a favor to a friend. It just went to show that no good deed went unpunished. She sheathed a cutting remark and took a breath as she surveyed the guy blocking her way.

At least six foot three or four, he was broad shouldered, narrow waisted and muscular. His physique belonged to an athlete, but the short-cropped blond hair and slate-gray eyes that possessed laser intensity screamed of a military background. The gray suit fit him perfectly and his silk tie was knotted precisely. The soft brown leather shoes held a shine. If he hadn't come across so blatantly obnoxious, he would have been attractive.

Eryn stood her ground defiantly. "Number one, I'm not a girl, I'm a woman. Number two, I'm the woman you're getting tonight."

The man kept his arms folded across his broad chest and didn't move. "Where's the other girl? The one we hired?"

Eryn couldn't believe the guy was being so particular. Renee had told her she'd never had a face-to-face with anyone

connected to the bachelor party and had only talked to someone named Toby. "She's not coming."

"Why?"

"She's sick. She called and asked me to cover your party."
The man's mouth tightened. "Not my party."

"Somehow, that doesn't surprise me. You don't seem like
the partying type." Or the marrying kind. But somewhere in
the back of Eryn's mind, that place where she kept foolish
thoughts, a bright *he's available* light just flashed on. She ignored it. The last thing she needed tonight was man trouble.
But ignoring the attractive male in front of her was hard.

The gray eyes narrowed. "Business must be good if you can
sass all your customers this way."

"I'm in a business where I'm not going to take a lot of crap
or disrespect. You can't pay me enough for that." Eryn hated
putting the gig at risk, because Renee was a single mom and
needed the money, and she'd said that bachelor parties could
pay really well. Only a really good friendship and a godson
would get Eryn so close to naked in a roomful of strange men.

"Cal, Cal. What are you doing, dude?" Another man,
younger than the guy blocking the door, stumbled over and
tried to lay an arm around the big man's shoulders. The effort
was wasted because he wasn't tall enough and he was amicably
drunk. He was dressed casually, jeans and sport jacket.

"Callan. Not Cal." The big man's voice remained soft but
carried definite authority. He was a man used to being obeyed.

"Okay…Callan." The newcomer drew back his arm. "But,
chill, dude. Don't hassle the stripper. We're all here for a good
time, and I paid good money for her."

Eryn counted to three. "I'm *not* a stripper." She didn't want
Renee or herself to be disrespected. Entertainment was a job, a
profession. The audience had to know its place up front. "I'm
here as an exotic entertainer. A dancer."

Back when she'd first arrived in Las Vegas, she'd worked as
a dancer for a while. Her career still suffered from that from
time to time as coworkers discovered her past, but that history

also allowed her to be good at her current profession. During her dancing days, she had always been very clear about the job description.

"And you paid for the performance, not me." She was also always very clear about what was paid for.

The drunken man smiled and shrugged. "Sure, sure, honey. No foul. Keep your shirt on. At least for now." He laughed at his own joke and glanced at the bigger man. The big man's sober expression never wavered and the man's good humor disappeared.

Callan didn't take his gaze from Eryn. He had deep, penetrating eyes. "She's not the entertainer you hired for this."

At first, Eryn thought the big man had referred to her as an entertainer as sarcasm, but there was no hint of that in his voice. She locked her gaze with his out of stubbornness and tried not to notice how beautiful his eyes were.

"That right?" The man shoved his hand out to Eryn and smiled. From the automatic way he smiled, Eryn felt certain he was a professional salesman. "I'm Toby. Best man. I'm paying for the party."

Eryn shifted her attention to Toby and put on a high-wattage smile. She could almost hear Renee whispering in her ear. *Always be polite to the guy paying the bill.* Renee had taught her that when she'd first gotten into the business. Plus, shifting her attention from tall, dark and obnoxious helped dial down the unexpected interest that had flared up.

"I'm Candy." She shifted her makeup kit and travel bag to her left hand and took Toby's hand in her right.

"Yes you are." Toby winked at her.

"But I'm not the entertainer you hired for the evening. My friend ended up sick a couple of hours ago. She asked me to cover for her."

"The other girl was blonde, right?"

Eryn ignored the gender terminology this time. The guy paying the bills was allowed certain liberties, and they stopped where she said they stopped. "My friend? Yes."

Toby leered at Callan. "You ask me, we're trading up. Daniel has a thing for blondes, which should make your sister happy. But I've always been partial to brunettes." He glanced back at Eryn. "And you're smoking hot, baby."

"Thanks." Eryn tried to sound like she meant it as she took her hand back from Toby. She held up her travel bag and makeup kit. "Do you have somewhere I can change?"

"Sure, sure. Right this way." Toby waved her inside the hotel suite.

Callan didn't move.

"C'mon, sarge, let the lady through. We don't have all night." Toby looked uncomfortable and not even close to being demanding. "After all, how many bachelor parties are we going to throw your future brother-in-law?"

With obvious reluctance, Callan stepped aside. Eryn slid by him with difficulty. Her shoulder brushed against his chest and discovered he was solid as a brick. Before she could completely ease by, he took her bag and kit from her with ease.

"Hey." Eryn reached for her things.

"Let me help you. Bedroom's this way." Somehow Callan turned his body so she couldn't get her property back, and in one long stride he was beyond her reach.

Eryn glared at Toby. "What's with this guy?"

"He's protective of his sister." Toby scratched the back of his neck and looked embarrassed.

"Is she here?"

"No, of course not. What kind of bachelor party would that be?" Bemused, Toby shook his head. "Callan's okay. Just…intense. Protective of his sister, protective of his future brother-in-law, I guess. Jenny, his sister, told me he was a control freak." He held up his hands. "But look, don't worry about things. You're going to come out of this okay. I'm a big tipper. So are the rest of Daniel's friends. This'll be fun."

You better hope so. Eryn wanted nothing more than to get her things back and leave, but Renee was counting on her.

Raising a child alone was expensive. Eryn walked through the expensive suite into the bedroom where Callan had disappeared.

When he reached the bedroom, Callan tossed the travel bag and makeup kit onto the bed. He didn't like surprises and he didn't like changes. Ops, even bachelor parties, were supposed to run smoothly. When things didn't run efficiently, situations got difficult. Or dangerous.

And the woman was definitely a surprise. She was just too competent, unafraid. Normally he liked that in a woman, but tonight she irritated him because he hadn't known she was coming and she didn't seem like the kind of woman who would come out of a cake in a roomful of horny, inebriated men she didn't know.

The makeup kit wasn't locked and he went through it quickly. He'd just picked up the locked travel bag when the woman walked in. She stopped in the doorway and gazed at the open makeup kit.

"I don't like people going through my things."

"I didn't think you would."

She was beautiful. At least five-ten with long legs, a trim build with generous curves, and a headful of curly dark brown hair. Her eyes were blue-green, as watchful as a cat's. Her mouth was a little too wide, but it looked fine on her. She wore a simple black dress that allowed her to fit in anywhere in Las Vegas's night scene.

Callan swallowed with difficulty and tried to drag his gaze from her, finally managing it with difficulty.

She crossed her arms. "The travel bag's locked."

"I noticed."

"Want me to open it for you?"

"Not necessary." Callan took out a lock pick set he'd already palmed and worked both locks. They popped open in seconds. Then he searched through the bag's contents. Panties, G-strings and an array of neon-colored sexy underthings filled the bag. Just to be sure, he felt the bag's lining as well. Lingering perfume and body powder filled his nose and made him think of how little flesh those lacy things covered.

He forced himself to think of the party as a security op. *You're in no man's land here, soldier. In enemy territory. Don't drop your guard.*

"I keep an inventory of everything in that bag, so don't think of taking any souvenirs."

The woman spoke calmly, but Callan knew she was angry. If he'd been in her shoes—stilettos, and expensive from the look of them—he'd have been angry, too. He shut down the trickle of guilt he was feeling. "Alphabetical or color-coded?"

"What?"

"The list. Is it alphabetical or color-coded?" She wasn't the only one that could be hard-nosed.

"Topographical. Based on how much they cover."

Despite his caution, the comment caught Callan off guard and made him smile. The brunette was quick. Then he scowled. He'd learned that quick-witted women could get a soldier dead in a heartbeat. He stepped away from the bed. "Okay, you can suit up." He headed for the door, but this time she blocked him. He looked down at her. "Either I can go and let you change, or I can stay and watch. Doesn't make any difference to me." But he was lying. He would have loved to have watched.

"It makes a difference to me." The woman stepped aside dismissively and entered the room. "You can leave."

Callan went out and headed for the big room where the party was going to take place. Daniel Steadman, his future brother-in-law, stood in the center of a dozen guys all getting happily plotzed at a wet bar set up in the corner of the big room.

Daniel was a nice guy. From the few times Callan had met him, Daniel was likable enough. But he wasn't the kind of man Callan generally associated with. All of the men in the room were involved in big business, and that made Callan feel awkward.

He reminded himself that he was doing this for Jenny. His

little sister had asked him to keep an eye out for Daniel, in case Toby and his friends got too wild. Jenny wasn't worried about other women, strippers or entertainers, but she was worried about everyone being in Las Vegas and so far from Dallas. Accidents happened. She'd wanted Callan to shepherd the group.

"Hey, Callan. You want a drink?" Daniel, tall and good-looking, his blond hair carefully cut and styled, waved at the bar.

Callan picked up his Diet Coke from the small table by the balcony doors. "I'm good. Thanks."

"Why don't you come over here and join us?"

"I'm gonna catch a breath of fresh air."

"Okay, bro. I just want you to have fun tonight. I promised Jenny I'd get you to loosen up. I'm kind of big on keeping promises to her."

Callan nodded. *Me, too.* He opened the balcony door, and went out into the night. He stared out at Las Vegas from the fourth floor. Standing there, he breathed in the stink of the city. Filth and raw sewage he was inured to, but he'd forgotten what smog and privileged pollutions were like. He'd been years from civilized areas, except for the few visits to check on Jenny. He'd come home for her high school graduation, college graduation, a handful of holidays and every now and then when he'd been out of action and recovering from wounds. Or planning a retaliatory move.

He sipped his drink and wondered why he was so on edge. Part of it had to do with Jenny marrying and the fact that he didn't know Daniel as well as he wanted to. But the biggest part of it was that he felt off his game, out of his terrain.

Despite that, he thought about the beautiful woman getting dressed in one of those sexy outfits he'd discovered in the travel bag. He'd liked the way she'd stood up to him and didn't back down, and he'd liked how she'd handled things when she'd found him going through her bags. She was cool and calm.

She was also unexpected, and that bothered him most of all. If there was one thing Callan had learned to hate, it was the unexpected.

"Look, I'm really sorry about that. Callan had no reason to treat you like that or go through your stuff."

"It's okay." Eryn made herself say that even though it wasn't okay. She was used to the wide gulf that separated the whales and major players in Las Vegas from everyone else. Her job at CyberStealth Security put her in that no man's land every day. High rollers or not, though, she didn't show up to get treated like garbage.

"He didn't mean anything by it." Toby looked uncomfortable.

Eryn looked at him and cocked a challenging eyebrow.

"He's just a careful guy."

"You mean, paranoid." Eryn had recognized it because that was how she played the game when she was on the job.

Toby shrugged. "Maybe. Tell you the truth, the guy creeps me out a little. I mean, I don't know him. He's Jenny's brother, but I haven't ever seen him until tonight."

"So what's his story?" Eryn refolded her underwear and placed them back in the bag.

"Don't know. He's some kind of soldier. He's been in Africa and the Middle East the past few years. I've heard he's a mercenary or something. You ask me, he's wired too tight." Toby looked at her. "He won't be a problem, though. One call to Jenny and she'll gentle him down."

"His sister can do that?" Personally, Eryn had her doubts. She would have bet that Callan was the kind of man no one could tame.

"That's what Daniel says."

"Ever seen her do it?"

"Nope."

Eryn nodded. "If he gets out of hand, hotel security is just a phone call away." She held up her cell. "I've got them on speed dial and I won't hesitate, bachelor party or not." She wiggled the phone. "Just so we're clear."

"It won't be a problem." Toby checked his watch. "I should probably let you get dressed." He hesitated a second, and Eryn knew he was contemplating adding a wisecrack, like *or help you get undressed,* but decided against it. Lucky him.

"That would be great."

"The cake's supposed to arrive in a few minutes." Toby pointed in the direction of the hallway. "Meet me outside when you're ready?"

"I will."

"Cool." Toby turned and left, closing the door behind him.

Eryn focused on her costumes. Calling the wispy bits of cloth costumes was more dignified than simply thinking of them as underwear. Calling them costumes made her feel more clothed. She wasn't overly conscientious of her body. Working this kind of job, she couldn't afford to be conscientious any more than she could afford to take her eyes off a principal, which was what CyberStealth called the clients they protected.

But as she surveyed her inventory, she couldn't forget about the big man. He'd thrown her with his casual disregard, and she hated that she was reacting to it as if he was a challenge. The problem was, he reminded her way too much of the jerks she had to put up with at CS Sec. She knew that a bachelor party wasn't going to require much in the way of dressing. The less, the better, in fact. But now she wanted something that would blow Callan's mind. Or at least his cool.

Looking over the selection, she wished she'd put in more thought about the event. But this had been such a no-brainer she hadn't thought about it. Reluctantly, she pulled out a white camisole with matching underthings and downy wings, and a scarlet two-piece ensemble with horns that left little to the imagination.

So which would fluster Callan more? Angel or devil? She pulled them up against her body in the full-length mirror on the wall, trying first one, then the other.

* * *

Toby was leaning against the wall in the hallway when Eryn found him. He had a beer bottle in one hand and was talking casually to a couple of hotel staff manning a pink and white cake on wheels. All three men stopped talking as Eryn stepped out into the hallway. She kept a satisfied smile from her face with effort. The other bodyguards and investigators at Cyber-Stealth couldn't generate *that* effect. Her looks were part of the package that repeat customers asked for, and it irritated the men she worked with.

"Wow." Toby's voice was hoarse. "And I do mean, *wow.*"

"Thank you." Eryn looked at the cake and saw that it had been outfitted with a selection of real cakes and desserts. "Are we ready?"

"Yeah." Toby gestured at the cake and the two hotel staff unlatched and opened it. There was plenty of room inside for her.

Eryn stepped forward. "I assume you're not going to simply unlatch the cake inside the suite. How do I get out?"

"Here." One of the men showed her how to unlatch the top and fold down a section of the cake. "Makes a step so you can get out without breaking your neck."

"Even in these heels?" Eryn lifted one of the deep red stilettos she wore.

"Don't know about heels."

Personally, Eryn didn't think the staff guy had even noticed she was wearing shoes. She'd chosen the red outfit, and it worked its magic on Toby and the hotel crew. "I'll manage." She stepped up and scrunched down inside the cake and adjusted her horns. "What's the groom-to-be's name?"

"Daniel. Daniel Steadman."

For the first time, the name sank into Eryn's mind. She'd been focused on tall, dark and distracting. "Daniel Steadman? As in Steadman Pharmaceuticals?"

The company was located in Dallas, which explained Toby's Texas accent. Steadman Pharmaceuticals had also been in the news lately as one of those companies making money when so many others were losing their shirts. They backed a NASCAR driver that had taken a couple of recent cups.

"Yeah. Just say the word. I'll introduce you inside, then you can come out of the cake."

"I'm ready." Eryn remained crouched inside the cake as she pulled the top down. A moment later, they were in motion, banging briefly against the door. Then she rolled to a stop.

"Hey, people, how about some entertainment?" Toby's voice boomed out over a PA system in the suite.

Eryn crouched inside the cake and felt her nervousness and reluctance melt away as adrenaline spilled through her body. Years of dance and gymnastics had trained away any performance anxiety she might have had, and she'd been just about as clothed. Martial arts and learning to deal with the whales and high rollers had sharpened her people skills.

"Let me present, the lovely *Candy!*"

Taking her cue, Eryn surged up, flipping the top layer of the cake back and standing tall. The second layer hit her almost across the knees. She threw her arms up and out as rock music with a heavy bass beat thundered from the suite's surround-sound system.

For one satisfying moment, Eryn spotted Callan on the other side of the room. The big man stood near the balcony doors, totally fixated on her, drinking in the devil costume with its high-collared vest that did nothing to cover the lacy pushup bra.

Then the cake detonated. Explosions ripped through the suite, accompanied by bright fireworks that spat sparks in all directions. Some of them singed Eryn's skin and she cried out in pain. Almost deaf, nearly blind and definitely disoriented, she held on to the sides of the cake in order to keep from falling.

At that moment, the suite's door crashed inward and a group of men wearing dark coveralls and ski masks invaded the room. They carried pistols and small machine guns.

A masked man grabbed one of the guys at the party and put a pistol to his head. Another masked man stepped forward and fired a burst that raked three of the walls and punched out glass from the balcony doors. The sound of the shots barely penetrated the cottony deafness that filled Eryn's ears.

"Get down on the floor! Do it now and you'll live!"

Chapter 2

Callan reached for the pistol that should have been holstered at his hip, but his fingertips brushed his slacks and closed on empty space. He hadn't brought a weapon to Las Vegas because security at the airports was so tight and too many questions would have been asked. The wedding was only going to take three days. He'd felt naked without the pistol, and now he felt vulnerable and helpless.

He clenched his empty hand into a fist. He focused, looking for options.

At the first explosion, he'd crouched, lifting his left arm to protect his face and save his eyesight, and taking two quick steps away from the window because broken glass often became shrapnel. The brief series of explosions echoed throughout the large room but the reinforced windows remained intact except for the bullet holes.

The attendees of the bachelor party reacted slowly, not certain what they were supposed to do. A few of them, prompted by television and action movies, fell to the ground and covered their heads with their arms or shoved their hands into the air in surrender. Partial deafness followed in the wake of the thunderous explosions and the gunfire.

Confused and uncertain, maybe a little drunk or stoned, a partygoer stood facing the men. His hands were over his head and he was crouched, but he hadn't gone to the floor. "Hey! Hey! Don't shoot!"

"I said, *get down!*" One of the men in black coveralls took a single step forward and kicked the man in the crotch. When the guy doubled over in pain, the invader slammed his machine pistol into the back of the man's head. The impact drove the man to the ground. The invader kicked the downed man in the forehead. The man quivered, then relaxed into unconsciousness.

Callan memorized as much information as he could. Ski masks covered the faces and hair. The coveralls masked body shapes. But he studied the weapons and the footwear. The machine pistols and handguns were expensive, and probably personal equipment. The men wouldn't throw them away. Stripping off the coveralls would give the men a different appearance almost immediately because they had clothes underneath. They weren't carrying extra footwear. They would keep the shoes. All of them wore the same black work boots.

A unit. Callan was certain of that. They dressed alike and they moved together, didn't talk much because they knew what they were doing. That could be a good thing, depending on what they were there to do. Callan hoped it was simple robbery. If Daniel and his friends didn't act stupid, they would all get to live.

Slowly, Callan spread his hands out and went down to the floor. Seven hostiles stood in the room at strategic points that offered everyone fields of fire. Cold anger stirred inside Callan despite his hopeful thought. The men were professional, at least to some degree, but they weren't willing to get too bloody with whatever they were doing. Otherwise they would have shot someone to prove they meant business.

Frustrated, his heart hammering, Callan watched in silence as the invaders swiftly worked the room.

"Billfolds and cash out on the floor." The speaker wore dark brown work boots that laced up to his midcalf. He'd been the one who had flattened the guy who'd moved too slowly. "We want your money and credit cards. All of it. Try anything stupid and you're going to leave the hotel in a body bag."

Callan reached inside his jacket and pulled out his wallet. He wasn't worried about the money. He kept only a little cash in the wallet. The rest was in his pocket and in his hotel room. He knew how to travel in potentially unfriendly environments, spread it out so it wasn't all seen or lost at one time. Despite the neon welcome mat in Vegas, he knew the city held predators. All metropolitan areas did. Small villages drew hunters as well, but they couldn't hide as quickly. He'd hunted predators nearly all his adult life.

He shoved the wallet beyond the reach of his hand. He pressed the left side of his face against the carpet. The smell of cleaning solvent burned his nostrils and almost made him sneeze. He watched, looking for the leader. Units tended to cycle around the guy in charge.

One of the invaders pulled a dark green plastic garbage bag from a coverall pocket. He handed his weapon to another man, then walked around the room collecting wallets and cash.

Callan drew a breath. The men were careful, seasoned. They knew how to work a hostile crowd. As the man with the bag made his rounds, another man crossed over to Daniel. The man hooked a big hand in the back of Daniel's shirt and yanked upward.

"Get up."

Scared, face red with panic, Daniel got up. He looked confused and lost, more like a boy than a man.

Callan pushed the thought from his mind. The assessment wasn't fair. He didn't know his sister's fiancé, but there was no way Daniel was prepared for what was taking place in the hotel room. Everyone in that room was afraid. Callan knew he was afraid, too, but he was better at working with his fear.

"What do you want?" Daniel spoke more calmly than Callan would have expected.

Good job, kid. Keep your head and you're going to be okay. Callan hoped that was true.

The man slapped Daniel's face hard enough to turn his head. Daniel stumbled but the man grabbed his shirt and pulled him up.

"Don't talk. Talking will only get you hurt. Do what I say when I say to do it."

Blood trickled from the corner of Daniel's mouth. He grabbed his attacker's arm and tried to kick the man in the groin.

Kid's got guts, but he's gonna get himself killed. Callan knotted a fist and worked hard to keep himself down. Bruises healed quickly enough.

The invader intercepted the kick on his thigh, then backhanded Daniel in the mouth. In the next instant, the man thrust the pistol into Daniel's bruised and battered face. The attacker rolled the hammer with his thumb.

Callan started to push himself up before he could check the movement. He froze when a gun barrel touched the back of his neck and shoved him down. The man hadn't shot Daniel. Callan quieted himself and waited.

The man drew the weapon back almost immediately, his point made. That was professional. Making contact with a prisoner was dangerous.

"Stay still, soldier boy, and you get to live through this."

They knew him. That fact sent an icy spike through Callan's gut. This wasn't just a random heist directed at a bachelor party. They knew who was going to be here, and who the guests were. That also meant the men weren't here just for the cash. He watched helplessly, feeling his captor's gaze. They'd put a man on just to watch him.

"You hear me, soldier boy?"

Controlling his fear and anger and frustration, Callan nodded. "Yeah. I hear you."

Before Daniel could recover from the rough treatment he'd received, the man turned him around. A second man joined the first. After the first man thrust his machine pistol under the second man's arm for safekeeping, he reached into one of the large coverall pockets and took out a roll of gray duct tape. He grabbed Daniel's arms and wound tape around his wrists.

Another strip of tape covered Daniel's bloody mouth. The next one covered his eyes.

Jenny's voice played in the back of Callan's mind. *Callan, I know this party isn't your kind of thing, but do it for me. I just want to make sure Daniel stays safe. Those guys can get kind of crazy, but they're fun crazy. Not bad guys.*

Callan clenched his hands into fists. Work through it. Learn what you can. They're a unit. Seven guys that you see, gotta be more working support and extraction. They're smart, efficient. They knew about the bachelor party. They knew who would be here. They knew about me.

Knowing about him was the biggest surprise. The work he did was kept off the grid. Not even Jenny knew everything. He'd kept that from her, not wanting his world to touch hers because he wanted her safe.

But he wasn't sure how many people Jenny had told about her big brother being a soldier. Daniel and Toby had known. Others at the party probably. The info wasn't secret, though Callan hadn't spent much time around his sister.

"Everybody listen." One of the invaders stepped into the center of the room. Although Callan couldn't see the man's mocking smile under the mask, he heard it in the man's voice. "Staying alive is really simple. You stay in this room after we leave, you live."

Callan's mind raced. He didn't want to lose sight of Daniel. Getting Daniel back would be harder if his location was unknown. Callan forced himself not to think that Daniel might not be coming back at all.

The man standing nearest the dancer gestured to her. "I want to take her."

A protective urge spread over Callan as he looked at the woman. She looked frozen, wide-eyed with fear, but she watched everything going on.

She should be more afraid. Callan seized that and kept hold

of the thought, turning it around in his mind. Was she a potential victim? Or a partner getting double-crossed? She didn't cower at all and watched everything.

The invader that had addressed the room shook his head. "She stays."

"She won't be a problem."

"If we're talking about her in the middle of this, she's already a problem."

The man cursed vehemently and shifted his attention to the dancer. "Sorry, baby. Gotta take a rain check on that. Woulda been fun."

Instantly Callan's suspicions cemented. The woman was part of the kidnapping. She'd changed places with the other performer and set off the flash-bangs.

"Let's move." The speaker waved toward the door and the exit began. A single man went first, followed by Daniel with two men flanking him. The other four followed in quick succession.

Callan shoved himself to his feet as soon as the door closed.

"Hey!" Toby waved at him wildly, never moving from the floor. "Get down! You heard what they said!"

Knowing fear was riding the man hard, Callan ignored him. The clock was in motion and every tick took Daniel farther away from him. Jenny loved Daniel and Callan didn't want to see his sister hurt.

The other guests had cell phones and were placing frantic calls to loved ones and to the police. Fearful conversations swelled and filled the room.

In four quick strides, Callan reached the booby-trapped cake. The woman was already on her feet. God, she was beautiful, seductive. Too bad Callan knew treachery always came in packages like that.

The woman looked far too calm and collected. That angered Callan.

She looked at him. "I need a phone. I left mine with my bags."

"You don't need a phone." Callan clamped a big hand on her wrist. "You're coming with me."

Her eyes blazed. "Coming with you where?"

"We're going to get your friends and I'm going to get Daniel back." Callan started for the door and yanked her after him.

Eryn couldn't pull free from Callan's greater size and strength. His hand felt like an iron band around her wrist. Her hearing still rang from the explosions, and adrenaline fueled her fight or flight instinct till she was just barely able to remain in control.

Your friends.

She couldn't believe that Callan could possibly think she was associated with the men who had just taken Daniel Steadman. Where was the line of logic for that? The man was out of his mind.

Then she remembered the kidnapper's efforts to get her to come with them. At the time, she'd been repulsed and afraid the answer would have been yes. She'd had no doubts about what the man intended.

Evidently Callan hadn't seen things the same way.

"I need a phone." Eryn tried to fight against him, but he dragged her after him like a rag doll without responding. She wanted to scream. She wanted to kick the back of his leg, trip him, then plant a roundhouse kick right into his head. Except that she felt certain the effort wouldn't have done any good. Callan was big and strong, and all she could do was delay both of them. For the moment, Daniel Steadman was in danger. "I can help if I get a phone."

Still on the move, his grip almost tight enough to cut off circulation, Callan pulled her in his wake. His long legs ate up the ground.

Like most of the members of the bachelor party, Toby still lay on the floor. He had his cell out now and unlocked the screen. Eryn leaned down and plucked the phone from his hands.

"Hey!" Toby grabbed at her frantically, but she was already out of his reach.

Even if Eryn had wanted to explain, there wasn't time. Callan was crossing the room in gigantic strides that caused her to take two to his every one. She had a hard time keeping up in the spike heels, but she managed.

She clutched the borrowed phone in her hand, then glanced at it briefly to make certain it was one she was familiar with. Knowing that the other guests would be calling the police and, hopefully, hotel security, she pulled up the phone's camera function.

Callan barreled through the door and out into the hallway. Eryn hesitated, thinking the gunmen would make good on their promise and leave someone out in the hallway. Irritably, like a cranky parent pulling at a stubborn child, Callan yanked her into motion again.

"Where are they taking Daniel?" His voice echoed like quiet thunder in the hallway.

"I don't know."

"They didn't tell you that part of the plan?"

She couldn't believe it and didn't even want to dignify the question with an answer, but she hoped he would listen. "They didn't tell me any part of the plan. I'm not—"

"You just climbed in the cake, set off the flash-bangs?"

Eryn cursed him inside her mind but kept her verbal anger inside because she knew voicing her observations wouldn't do any good. Callan was reacting emotionally, obviously worried about the kidnap victim. She remembered what Toby had told her about Callan being overly protective of his sister and how that spread to other people in her life.

She tried again. "I'm not part of this."

Callan shot her a hard-eyed look filled with determination and resolve. That look cut right through her. "You can lie to the police. Not me."

"I'm not lying."

Switching his attention back to the hallway again, Callan kept moving. "They knew about Daniel."

"The wedding's probably in the papers. It wouldn't take a rocket scientist to figure there might be a party in the same hotel where the wedding was going to take place."

He grimaced. "They knew about me."

"Knew what?"

"Don't play games."

"I don't know anything about you."

"They did. You didn't have to. All you had to do was set off the cake."

Eryn opened her mouth to protest at the same time Callan flicked out a hand and set off the fire alarm on the wall. Warning Klaxons roared to life and pierced the cotton in her ears. Callan glanced at the elevator bank at the next hallway.

Watching the digital numbers on all the cages dropping steadily and uniformly, Eryn suddenly understood the move. With the fire alarm engaged, all the elevators would descend to the first floor without stopping. If the kidnappers had taken the elevators, they would be momentarily trapped.

Room doors opened along the hallway as guests came out. "Is there a fire?"

"Is that the fire alarm?"

Callan brushed through the people as he headed for the emergency exit.

Impressed, Eryn looked at him. "You did that so more people would be around to identify the people who took Daniel." The move was clever and she instantly respected it. She hadn't thought of that, but she would definitely file it away. "Those guys will dump the masks and coveralls, but they can't dump the hostage. You're hoping you can get an ID from a bystander."

Callan glared at her, then he opened the emergency exit door and dragged her through. Traversing the stairs was a lot trickier in heels than simply keeping up with Callan. She stumbled and fell repeatedly, always bumping up against that rock-hard back just ahead of her. Moving swiftly, he grabbed her again and again, righting her and keeping her moving. Her feet ached with the constant stress of navigating the steps and she hoped she didn't turn an ankle.

The bachelor party had been on the fourth floor. Four flights of stairs later, Eryn thought they were going to enter the lobby again. Instead, Callan continued the descent into the underground parking garage.

"The elevators stop at the first floor." Eryn turned the corner on the landing and headed down the stairs after Callan. The parking garage door was straight ahead.

"Did they plan on taking the elevator?"

"I don't know."

Callan shook his head. "They wouldn't have taken the elevators. Not with Daniel. He'd be too easy to identify, and then the men who had taken him could be identified as well."

Eryn knew that was true. Hotel security kept cameras in all the elevators. She looked at Callan's profile, so hard it could have been carved from granite, and wondered who he was and how he knew all the things he did.

He was calm and in control. Not only that, he wasn't even breathing hard from the pell-mell rush down the stairs. He reached for the knob and opened the door.

Car engines and voices echoed inside the cavernous parking garage. The temperature changed immediately from cool to muggy despite the fact that night had fallen over Vegas. The lows in August usually were in the seventies.

While Callan came to a dead stop and looked around like a hound on the hunt, Eryn took a deep breath filled with carbon monoxide and burned oil. Callan pulled her around to look at him.

"What are they driving?"

"I don't know."

"Where are they taking Daniel?"

"Look, you've got this all wrong. I'm not—"

Thirty yards away, the side door of a cargo van slid open

with a grating shrill. Interior light from the vehicle spilled out onto the parking garage and lit up Daniel Steadman and his captors. The men still wore the black coveralls. The van gaped emptily as one of the men shoved Daniel inside.

Eryn lifted the cell, pointed it at the van, and started taking digital images. The phone was expensive. She hoped the camera utility was, too, but it wouldn't compare to a 35mm SLR. Still, there might be something recoverable later. She only managed three images in quick succession before Callan jerked her into motion.

The men climbed into the van, but not before one of them spotted Callan and Eryn. He pointed and called out a warning to one of the other men. He grabbed for the machine pistol hanging from a sling on his side.

"What are you doing?" Eryn pulled at her arm, certain they were about a heartbeat from getting shot.

"Getting Daniel."

"You're going to get shot. You're going to get *us* shot."

Twenty yards out, Callan never broke his stride. Eryn had seen few men with that kind of single-minded intensity. Her father was one of them, and she respected him. But running into a group of armed men was suicidal.

"They didn't shoot anyone upstairs. Maybe they're not shooters."

"They will shoot you. They'll shoot me."

Callan's grip tightened on her wrist. "I thought you said you didn't know these guys."

"I don't."

"Then you don't know if they're really willing to kill someone."

Two of the men lifted their machine pistols from inside the van. The engine caught and the driver roared backward, then braked forcefully to a stop. The men took aim, cursing loudly at the driver.

Unwilling to run into a hail of bullets to prove Callan wrong, Eryn kicked his leg out from under him and threw herself against him. She was surprised when the ploy worked. They fell hard onto the parking garage's cement floor just as bullets struck sparks from the smooth surface and whined off into the parking garage. Bullets hammered out glass from a nearby Suburban and punched holes in the body.

The impact knocked the wind from Eryn's lungs. She lay helpless and watched as the van roared straight at where she lay on top of Callan. The headlights flicked on and the vehicle looked like some hollow-eyed monster bearing down on them. The gunners inside the van kept firing.

Bullets slammed into nearby vehicles. Pockmarks appeared in spiderweb windows. Sparks leaped from fenders as some of the rounds ricocheted. Car alarms screeched to strident life and a light show from the stricken vehicles ignited. A cry of pain from another area of the garage caught Eryn's attention.

Lying on her side, Eryn tried to push herself up and reach for Callan, certain they would never get clear. He roped an arm around her and flipped himself on top of her. His hard body pressed against her and for a moment her senses swam with the presence of him. Despite the motor smells beaten into the garage, she smelled him, inhaled the musk mixed with some kind of cologne that seemed familiar but was so different on him. His free hand slid up her spine and cupped the back of her head protectively as he rolled.

Eryn realized he was trying to maneuver them from the path of the advancing van but didn't know if there was enough time. She lay pliantly against him and wrapped her arms under and over his, holding on so tight it was like they were one body. They rolled once more and the van's tires sped by only inches away. The heat of the vehicle and the stink of the exhaust washed over them as another fusillade of bullets chopped into nearby cars.

Stunned, not believing she was still alive—or in Callan's arms, Eryn stared up into his slate-gray eyes. Then he released her and surged to his feet like a big cat, the motion so smooth she couldn't see the parts of it. He was suddenly just standing.

Eryn sat up, not sure if she could trust her trembling knees. The adrenaline still flooded her system and left her shaky. She'd never come so close to being killed. She looked across the garage and saw a guy on the ground. Just a tourist in the wrong place at the wrong time. Miraculously, she'd managed to hang on to the cell phone and it wasn't broken. She called 911 to get an ambulance to him, even knowing he wasn't alive.

At the end of the parking garage, the van cut the corner sharply and pulled into the exit lane. The tires shrilled against the pavement.

For a moment Callan stared after the fleeing vehicle, hard and cold as stone. Then he wheeled on her. "You let them get away."

Chapter 3

Eryn stared at Callan, not believing what she'd just heard. Angry, clad in a skimpy costume, still afraid and buzzing with adrenaline, she stood on trembling legs. Despite their size difference and the volatile circumstances, she refused to back down from him.

"I let them get away?" Eryn's words came out harsh and angry as she leaned toward Callan. "You ass! I just saved your life!"

"I had everything under control."

"What were you going to do? Tackle that van?" Eryn snorted sarcastically, her anger momentarily overriding her fear. "I'm sure that would have worked out really well for you. They'd have peeled you off the grill. But that would have made the car easier to identify. Maybe I should have let you go."

The planes of his face hardened. "Who are those guys? Who took Daniel?"

"I don't *know!*" Eryn sipped a deep breath and looked at the phone. She pulled up the shots she'd taken, then triggered the email function and sent them to her phone back in the hotel room and to her home computer.

"Are you calling them?" Callan reached for the phone.

Eryn turned sideways and threw her shoulder into the big man's arms to block the grab. "No. I'm securing evidence. Back off."

"What evidence?"

This time his grab was too quick for her and he snatched the phone from her hand while she'd been focused on sending the images. She resisted the impulse to try to get the phone back. Unless she had a baseball bat or a Taser, that wasn't going to happen until he was ready to hand it over.

"What is this?" Callan peered at the phone screen.

"What does it look like?"

"You took pictures of the van?" He studied her with hard-edged curiosity.

"Yes. If we get lucky, maybe we can enlarge those images and read the plates."

He flicked his gaze back to the image and stared hard at it, as if memorizing every detail. "They won't have used their own vehicle. They were too professional." He spoke more to himself than to her.

"What makes you so sure?" The thought that the kidnappers had stolen the van had crossed Eryn's mind. But the pictures at least gave them something to work with. Then she caught herself and couldn't believe how easily she'd transitioned to "them" instead of her.

"They were professionals."

"And you know professionals."

His voice turned cold and flat. "Yeah, I know professionals."

Eryn folded her arms across her chest and stared at him. For the first time she noticed the scars on his hand and neck. They were hard and violent, some of them recent and not the result of childhood misadventure.

Callan looked at her. Even while he'd been studying the images on the phone screen, he'd never taken his attention wholly from her. "Is this the only picture?"

"Image. No, it's not."

"How many more?"

"Three altogether."

"Show me the others." He handed her the phone.

Taking the phone, Eryn flipped through the three images. She went one more image than expected and saw a picture of her stepping into the cake. It had been taken from behind. Evidently Toby had snapped her in the hallway.

Callan took back the phone and flipped through the images the way Eryn had. He was a quick learner. "Can you save these pictures?"

"Images. I already have."

"How?"

"I sent them to my phone and home computer."

"This isn't your phone."

"What gave it away? The fact that I couldn't have taken that shot of myself? Or the fact that I wouldn't have taken that particular shot?"

"The fact that the underwear you have on is too skimpy to have concealed this phone."

The comment made Eryn immediately feel uncomfortable. But she was almost scandalized at the satisfaction she took in knowing that Callan had noticed how she'd been dressed. Or, rather, undressed. Self-consciously, she covered herself with an arm, clinging to her shoulder with her hand.

"It's Toby's phone. I took it on the way out of the room." Eryn knew from the wary glint in his eyes that she had surprised him. He'd underestimated her, and now he knew that he had on several levels.

Callan studied her. "Why did you take these pictures?"

"To give to the police."

He stared at her harder and she found it difficult to meet his gaze.

"I'm not working with them." She was surprised at how much she cared that he believed her. Her reaction was foolish, and it was wasted. One thing she knew for sure about Callan was that he was pigheaded.

Stubbornly, he shook his head. "You were a last-minute substitution. No way that wouldn't be suspect. The police are going to think the same thing."

"Did you think maybe me being there was a surprise to those guys, too?" Still, she knew he had a valid point. The investigating detectives were going to be all over her.

Callan growled a little but appeared to consider the possibility. "Maybe the girl you replaced was in on the kidnapping. She could have set you up."

Eryn cursed to herself. The last thing she wanted to do was get Renee involved in this. "No."

"Maybe she got cold feet and left you hung out to dry."

"No, that's not what happened. I stepped in for a friend. Someone I've known for years. She got sick and needed someone to take her place for this job. She couldn't afford to miss out on the money." As she said that, Eryn felt bad. With the way things had gone down, Renee was still going to come up short. But that would be okay. Between them they would work things out. Renee just liked to be independent.

"Why did that guy want to take you with him?"

Thinking of how the man had eyed her, the hunger in his dark eyes, Eryn suddenly felt insecure about her near-nudity. The devil costume didn't cover much and the parking garage was cold. She shuddered. "I'd rather not think about it."

After a moment, Callan nodded. He slipped off his suit coat and draped it over her shoulders. The coat was scuffed and dirty from the scramble across the parking garage pavement, but it was warm and hung nearly down to her knees.

"Thanks."

Sirens screamed to life and thundered into the parking garage.

"The police are coming." Eryn relaxed a little. She felt bad that Daniel Steadman wasn't safe, but she was glad she was.

Callan gripped her elbow and yanked her into motion again. She pulled back against him. He tightened his grip and pulled harder. He growled irritably. "C'mon."

"C'mon where?"

"I don't want to get caught up with the police."

"Why?" For the first time Eryn wondered if Callan might

be dangerous. Not just physically dangerous, because she was certain he was that, but dangerous in a criminal sense. Toby had said that Callan was a soldier, but people thought mercenaries were soldiers, too. Many of them had been. Too many private armies were springing up around the globe, and not all of those people were nice. Maybe Callan had something to hide.

"Because I'm going to get Daniel back."

"The police can help." Eryn dug in her heels, but Callan pulled her toward the emergency exit all the same.

"Working with the police on this kidnapping would be like swimming in quicksand. They take too long to form up, think too much before they act. Since this is a kidnapping and Daniel is from out of state, and they killed that guy in the garage, the FBI is going to get called in. Especially because of who his family is. That'll slow Daniel's rescue down even more. He'll be dead if they get too involved."

Eryn knew that was true. She'd never been directly involved in a kidnapping before, but her company had. Usually those crimes ended tragically.

"You're one man."

He looked at her but smiled grimly. "Yeah, but I can do this. I've done it before."

Looking at him, staring into those hard, slate-gray eyes, Eryn believed him—but only for a moment. The bottom line was that Daniel Steadman had been taken by professionals. Callan had acknowledged that himself. But she knew he was going to try to get Daniel back.

She also knew that he wasn't going to ask her for help. Once he got his hands on the images, he'd take up the hunt by himself. Getting around Las Vegas was hard. "When was the last time you were in Vegas?"

He smiled a little. "First time."

And navigating the city if he hadn't been here before was going to be next to impossible. The sirens closed in as Eryn stared at him and considered what he was proposing to do. "You can't do this by yourself. Not in a city you don't know."

"My kid sister loves this guy. I'm not going to sit this one out while he gets flushed down the toilet because of bureaucracy." Callan took a quick breath. "The men who took him knew who I was. Inside that room, they had a guy on me. They figured if there was any trouble coming, I was the guy going to give it."

Thinking of the way Callan had rushed at the van despite the gunners, Eryn silently agreed. He *was* trouble.

"Those guys had an inside person." Callan went on in a calm voice. "If it wasn't you—"

"It wasn't." Eryn glared at him.

Callan ignored her response. "—then it's someone else. If it's someone else, then that person is going to be in the middle of the police and FBI investigation. They're going to know every move the police and the FBI make. That'll get Daniel killed. This is about money. They're going to have to move quickly."

"You don't know this is about money."

He flicked a narrow-eyed glance at her. "Daniel's heir to a pharmaceutical empire. This is about money."

"Whoever took him could have taken him for leverage."

That caught his attention. "What do you mean?"

"Corporate buyout. Corporate merger. Research and development. A play for contracts. Revenge. You can't narrow your focus like that." Eryn couldn't believe so many possibilities presented themselves to her so quickly.

Callan's suspicion returned. "How do you know all this?"

"This is Vegas. People who come here are high rollers. Corporate executives who like to play hard but never stray far from the business field. You get to that level, it's all about action. It doesn't matter if it's in the boardroom, on Wall Street or on the tables. They have to get their juice."

"Doesn't matter what this is about. I'm going to get Daniel

back. Whoever sold him out is going to be in a position to look over the shoulders of the law enforcement people."

"You don't know that."

"I do."

Although she wanted to believe that someone inside the group of partygoers colluding with the kidnappers was simply conspiracy paranoia, Eryn knew it was likely true. She'd seen the man assigned to Callan. He'd gone straight to Callan and hadn't hesitated to shove his pistol into the back of Callan's neck.

"Getting Daniel back safely is going to take someone from outside law enforcement. Someone moving quickly." Callan paused, then his voice turned cold. "And someone who won't hold back when the time comes."

"What do you mean?"

Before Callan could respond, if he was going to, the fire escape door exploded open and a group of hotel security guards pushed into the parking garage brandishing weapons. They fanned out immediately, one stopping by the body on the ground and took up positions as the first LVPD police car screeched to a stop in front of them. The red and blue lights whirled over the immediate scene, painting it in garish shadows.

Callan wrapped his jacket around Eryn's shoulders and herded her toward the stairwell at the other end of the parking garage. "I need those pictures. After that, you're out of this. I promise. You can do whatever you want. But I have to help Jenny. I promised."

The forceful emotion in his words carried pain and concern. Eryn was surprised to hear it, but in the end that was what decided her. She nodded and went with him, skirting parked cars and staying in the darkness.

Callan took the lead up the stairwell and shielded the woman with his body. He pushed hard, and this time he realized she was in heels. Her ability to keep up surprised him. Three hotel security guards came down and stopped them on the stairs.

One of the security men pushed a hand against Callan's broad chest. Callan barely managed to quell the reflex to break the man's fingers and chop him in the throat. "Who are you?"

Before Callan could respond, the woman peered around his shoulder. "It's crazy out there. Guys with guns. Looked like some kind of drive-by. I think they're still out there. It's a good thing you guys got here. You should be able to catch them."

The cacophony of car alarms echoed into the stairwell as the door below opened again.

The security guard shifted his attention to the woman. "Did you see who they were?"

"No. We were just getting into our car when it started. I told George we were safer inside the hotel."

"You're probably right. I need your names."

"Darbinson. Room twenty-two fourteen. George and Kelli. We're still checked in. We were going out for dinner until all that happened."

The security guard nodded. "You folks get to your room. Someone will probably be along to talk to you."

"Okay, thanks. You guys be careful." Eryn flashed them a smile.

Callan was surprised by how quickly the woman had defused the situation by shifting the security guards from interrogators to protectors and potential heroes. But the ease that she accomplished that also strengthened his ebbing suspicions. She was too quick, too ready with a lie. A normal person off the street didn't lie like that.

But the security guards went on their way.

She looked up at him, obviously expecting some acknowledgement of her feat.

"Take off your shoes."

An angry frown tightened her blue-green eyes. "What?"

"Your shoes. Take them off. It's a wonder you haven't broken your neck."

"I don't need to—"

Kneeling quickly, Callan grabbed one of her toned calves and lifted her foot from the ground. She stumbled and almost lost her balance. He was too aware of the warm flesh in his hand and his chest suddenly felt too tight. The contact was electric and he wanted to skate his fingers along her calf some more. Instead, he cupped her raised foot with his other hand and stripped the shoe.

"Don't—"

Shifting legs, trying to keep the feel of her from his mind, Callan pulled off the other shoe, leaving it on the ground by the other. He stood and faced her glare. "Things are going to happen fast now. If I have to run, I want you able to keep up with me."

"I can keep up with you. I could have done it in heels, too." Her jaw jutted angrily.

Seeing the competitive, daring gleam in her eyes almost made Callan laugh. Under other circumstances he would have. Instead, he gripped her by the arm and pulled her toward the next flight of stairs.

She squirmed in his grip, twisted her wrist toward his thumb the way most martial arts taught someone to counter a hold, and broke free. For a moment Callan thought she was going to try to run. To his surprise, she reached down and hooked her fingers through the straps of the heels.

She held them up to display. "Manolo Blahniks. You don't leave Manolo Blahniks behind. Now let's go." She dashed past him, easily taking the steps three at a time.

She was fast. Callan realized that by the time he hit the top of the stairs. In the tight confines of the stairwell, she was pulling ahead of him because his size and weight worked against him. Muscle became a burden in the tight turns. In a straightaway run he felt he could have beaten her. Or at least kept up. He was also aware of her only inches in front of his face. The glimpses of red silk beneath his jacket threatened to drive him crazy.

Focus, Callan. He took in a deep breath and pushed it out, turning his thoughts to Daniel Steadman and Jenny. Callan knew he would have to talk to his sister and he was dreading that conversation.

He reached the fourth-floor landing three steps behind her. She waited for him at the door.

"Catch your breath. They probably have hotel security in the room now. We don't want to attract any more attention than we have to."

Callan wanted to argue with her and tell her that his breathing was just fine. Instead, he focused on her words. "That costume is going to draw a lot of attention."

"This is Vegas. A lot happens in Vegas. You can look and dress any way you want to. Just don't act suspicious." She frowned at him. "Why did you want to come back here?"

"I've got to get my things from my room."

"I thought you were in a hurry."

"If I'm going to look for these guys, I'm going to need money. I also need to get out of these clothes, change my appearance. That's all in my room. I'm at the end of the hall."

She nodded and looked at him. "Ready?"

"Yeah. Me first. In case there's trouble." Callan stepped in front of her, opened the door, and passed into the hallway.

Pulse pounding, Eryn trailed a step behind and to Callan's right. She took advantage of his size to hide from the other people filling the hallway. Even with the coat, the devil costume marked her immediately if anyone was looking for her. She didn't want people remembering her or, worse, pointing her out to investigators and security staff.

The party had boiled out into the hallway. Dozens of half-drunken young men talked and gestured, replaying everything that had just happened. Their voices were loud and histrionic. Plainclothes hotel security, marked by the walkie-talkies they carried, moved among the group. The security staff took down names and secured the scene.

Callan cut through them. He was big and broad, but he moved like a tiger. She'd been hard-pressed to gain any distance on him in the stairwell. Given his size and intensity, she thought he'd stand out immediately. But no one noticed him for more than a second, all of them consumed with their stories and the danger that had just passed. As she watched, she realized that Callan never made more than fleeting eye contact, kept a smile on his face and never broke stride, moving quickly without giving the appearance of doing so.

He stopped at the doorway to the room where Eryn had dressed. He tried the door and found it locked. He frowned and turned to Eryn.

Stepping past him, Eryn knocked on the door. Before she finished, the phone in her hand buzzed for attention. Out of habit, she glanced at the screen.

The image of a beautiful woman filled the screen. She had a heart-shaped face, lavender eyes and a small mouth. Cinnamon tresses fell over her bare shoulders. She held a bright red rose in one hand that almost touched the cleft in her chin. The image was glamour shot, an expensive makeover judging from the cosmetics, color and smoky background. A name flashed underneath: Sierra.

Eryn figured Toby was the kind to collect the phone numbers of a lot of women with one name.

Callan peered at the screen. "That's Toby's sister."

"Oh." Eryn felt guilty for her earlier thought when she realized Toby's sister was probably worried and calling to check on her brother. She accepted the call. The least she could do after purloining the phone was let Toby's sister know he was okay. "Hello."

"Who is this?" The feminine voice was edgy and demanding, used to wielding authority.

"Eryn."

"I know three Erins. Which are you?"

"I'm one that you don't know."

"What are you doing with Toby's phone?"

"I borrowed it."

"I heard what happened at the party and I wanted to make certain Toby was all right."

"He's fine." Eryn glanced back down the hall where Toby talked loudly to a security guard. "He's kind of busy at the minute talking to the hotel security staff."

"Have him call me. Soon."

The hotel door opened and revealed one of the guests. His eyes widened as Callan planted a big hand against the door and forced it farther open.

"I'll have Toby get in touch with you as soon as he's free." But Eryn was speaking into a dead connection. The woman had hung up. Turning her thoughts back to the moment, Eryn followed Callan into the room.

Chapter 4

"Hey." The guy backpedaled into the room just ahead of Callan. "Callan Storm, right? Jenny's brother?"

"Yeah." Callan surveyed the room and crossed to the bed where Eryn's things lay.

Eryn walked to the bed, opened her overnight bag, got her purse out and checked her cell. The images she'd sent from Toby's phone had come through perfectly.

"Has hotel security been in here?" Callan focused on the guy in the room.

"No." Guilt stained the man's features.

"What are you doing here?"

Eryn smiled at that. Evidently suspicion was hardwired into Callan's psyche, but the guy was tripping her radar as well.

The man looked guilty. "Had to get rid of something." He shrugged nervously. "Wasn't anything big, but I didn't want to take the chance. Didn't want to get busted by the cops."

Eryn shook her head. Apparently not all of Daniel Steadman's acquaintances were squeaky clean. That knowledge made her wonder about Daniel Steadman and Callan's sister. She had to wonder just how wild they were and if an alternative lifestyle directly impacted what had happened tonight.

Silently, she chastised herself. She had no right to judge, and the guys had shot up the parking garage and killed an innocent bystander without flinching. Not all of her acquaintances were squeaky clean, either. And her past as an exotic dancer, no matter how short, wouldn't have cut it with her hometown in Fallon even as close as it was to Las Vegas. Her father was a carpenter and her mother was a schoolteacher. She hadn't hidden her job from them and it had caused some stress. But she was their only child and forgiveness always came.

No, the trouble Daniel Steadman was currently in had to be way past anything he'd expected.

She went through her clothing, thankful the outfit she came in was practical enough. Coffee-bean-colored boot-cut stretch pants she could move in, a chestnut-colored three-quarter sleeve draped surplice shirt and brown Rockport Addison short boots she'd intended to wear home after the job. The clothes would blend with the Strip night crowd and the boots were sturdy enough to hold up under duress.

Callan switched his gaze to her. "I need those pictures."

"I'm going with you." Eryn didn't relish spending the evening getting grilled by police officers. With as many people as there were involved with the kidnapping, investigators would waste hours just processing the attendees. Callan was right about that.

And family was important. Even though Callan's sister wasn't in direct danger, Jenny Storm was going to be hurt if something happened to her fiancé. Eryn didn't want that to happen for any of them. One of the main reasons she'd gotten involved in security work was to protect people. She still had nightmares about Megan's death. Someone should have helped her, but no one had.

Besides, whatever information they got from the images of the van might play out in minutes. Furthermore, if she could get away clean, without anyone from CS Sec finding out about her moonlighting for Renee, Eryn preferred that. Toby had never gotten her real name, and Renee took jobs through a booking service that protected the names of the performers.

The investigators might not even try to find out who the woman in the cake had been—unless they jumped onto the same wrong assumption Callan had. Eryn took a deep breath and told herself that the kidnapping would be resolved by then. The police—the FBI—would stop looking. All she had to do was get out of the building and she'd be clear.

Callan scowled. "You're not going with me."

"Fine. You're going with me." Before he could stop her, Eryn stepped into the bathroom, locked the door and waited to see if Callan would tear the door off the hinges. She heard him pace outside for a moment, maybe growl a little, but he stayed on the other side of the door.

Eryn undressed and dressed quickly. She dropped the skimpy attire into her purse, washed the exotic makeup from her face, and expertly glossed her lips and worked magic with a concealer. She moussed her collar-length hair and let it fall straight and professional, getting rid of the body she'd worked hard to infuse it with earlier. When she checked her reflection in the mirror, she was happy to see that a much different person looked back at her. She felt certain she could fade into the background of the hotel and leave without incident.

But there was one other stop she needed to make if she intended to follow through on her impromptu investigation. Callan wouldn't like it. She didn't, either, because it would leave her more exposed than ever.

When she opened the door, Callan spun on her. His irritation and stern features froze for just a moment, then he looked surprised.

The other man in the room wasn't so silent. "Wow. You look different."

Eryn didn't respond. She deleted the images she'd taken from the memory card, wiped the phone clean of her fingerprints and Callan's with a tissue, then handed Toby's cell to man. "Get this to Toby. Tell him his sister called and she's worried."

"Sierra? Sure." The man nodded, still not taking his eyes from Eryn. "You know, you look even hotter now."

Terrific. She checked her phone again, making sure she had the images she'd sent from Toby's phone. Then she grabbed her travel bag and makeup kit from the bed.

Callan blocked the doorway. "Two things. You're not going with me. And I need those pictures."

She returned his glare with one of her own. "Two things. You try to get out of here without me and I blow the whistle to the hotel security." She took a breath, testing her resolve and discovering—without surprise—that she still couldn't shake it. "I also think you're right about Daniel Steadman's kidnapping being an inside job. Which means I'm going to try to help you."

"I don't need you tagging along."

"If I let you walk away, that makes me responsible."

"For what?"

"For anything stupid that you do." She eyed him levelly. "That's the deal, soldier. Take it or leave it."

Callan growled in the back of his throat and the sound thrilled through Eryn in ways she'd never experienced. She put the reaction down to adrenaline, to nearly dying, at being happy to still be alive. And then she wondered why she was in such a hurry to continue hanging around Callan Storm when bad things were sure to happen. At the very least her private security license was on the line, and she'd worked hard to get it.

She held her gaze steady, not showing any of her inner turmoil. "Clock's ticking."

"Fine." From Callan's abrasive tone, the answer was anything but fine. He reached out for her travel bag. She pulled it away, but he caught it and took hold. "If you're carrying both bags while I'm walking around empty-handed, that's going to draw attention."

Reluctantly, but knowing that what he said was true, Eryn

let him have the bag. She wasn't happy about any concession she made toward him.

"Let's go." He opened the door and they went into the hallway.

As he followed the woman down the stairwell, Callan cursed to himself. He couldn't believe she'd insisted on coming along. She had no vested interest in anything that was taking place, despite her argument that she would somehow be held "responsible."

His lack of cell phone experience was a drawback. He'd have to remedy that at his first opportunity, but it wasn't likely to be tonight. She turned and headed down the hallway toward his room. He studied her as he matched her determined stride. So what was her angle? Everybody had one, and they tended to be selfish.

He gave himself a mental shake. *Roll with it. For the moment you need her. She has intel that you need. Once you get it, you can flush her and drop her like a rock.*

The past few years, his missions had been in Afghanistan and Africa, in back areas that were barely listed on the map. Cell phones would have drawn enemy attention at once. He'd made do with human intelligence after the parameters of the missions had been drawn, operating independently behind enemy lines with a handful of people that might or might not betray him. He was currently functioning out of his depth, in foreign terrain, and he knew it.

He used his keycard on the door to his room and went inside. Behind him, the woman reached for the light. He caught her hand and stopped her.

"Leave the light off."

Through her hand, he felt her body go tense. It took him a moment to remember to release her. Touching her sent an electrical current through him that he would have sworn he'd never before experienced. He didn't know what it was about the woman that affected him so much, but he disliked it. She infuriated him on so many levels. Yet when he touched her, he seemed to get brain-locked.

Stupid. Pay attention. You need to help Daniel.

Callan turned away from her, grateful that the room was dark so she couldn't see his face, because he didn't know what she might see there. "Security may check to see if I'm here. If they see a light, they'll know I'm around."

"Okay." She didn't sound sure of herself. The darkness in the room was nearly complete except for the neon glow from the Strip filtering around the heavy drapes.

Reaching into his pocket, Callan took out the small Mini Maglite he usually carried. A professional soldier who habitually risked his life never went anywhere without light, a way of making fire and a knife. Antitank weaponry and an escape helicopter were much harder to pack. He had all of those basic things, though the Swiss Tinker blade he carried wouldn't count much as armament facing automatic weapons.

He switched the light on and directed the white light against the ceiling. He dialed the wattage down to a glow that barely reflected against the overhead tiles and only just lifted their silhouettes from the darkness.

"Here." He handed the light to the woman. "Give me a minute to get dressed." Before she could respond, he turned and crossed to the small closet.

He flung the door open, took out a pair of khaki cargo pants, a burgundy pullover and a pair of GORE-TEX hiking boots he'd broken in. He left the rest of the clothes hanging. The room was rented for two more days—for the wedding tomorrow night and one more day. He wasn't going to need anything else from there until he got Daniel back to Jenny.

He entered the bathroom and changed out of his clothing.

At first Eryn thought Callan had left the bathroom door ajar by mistake. Then, curious, she'd peered through the opening and realized she could see the mirror. And in the mirror, she saw his reflection as he stood behind the door and changed clothing. She also realized then that he'd left the door open on purpose. He'd given her the Mini Maglite for the same reason.

Just as she could see him, he could see her. He was watching her, making certain she didn't leave. His slate-gray eyes looked at her intently. Her image was clearer due to the flashlight, but there was still enough illumination to see him.

That made Eryn angrier. She didn't know where he thought she would go. And he'd practically been shoving her out the door. If she didn't have the images he wanted, she wouldn't be there now. She thought about extinguishing the light out of spite, just to see if she could get a reaction out of him.

But turning the flashlight off would have plunged the bathroom into darkness. He'd still know if she left when the door opened. She told herself that keeping the light on was just to keep the peace, but she knew she liked the way the soft glow played over his body.

She couldn't see much of him, but it was enough to set her heart racing a little. The response bothered her, especially given everything that was currently going on.

Callan was lean, but his upper body packed muscle. The light played over his broad shoulders, deep chest and biceps as they bunched when he moved. There were scars, too, faded things that she couldn't quite make out. His white boxer briefs stood out against the bronze skin. He was dark all over, like he lived out in the elements. The coloration wasn't the result of a tanning booth. Wherever Callan was from, he was exposed a lot.

He pulled his pants on, covering his near nakedness, and Eryn had to take a breath. Her face felt hot, but she knew she wasn't embarrassed. Then she realized she was, over her reaction, though, not because she'd seen him nearly stripped. She'd worked protection for female clients at Chippendales shows, had seen a lot more skin under definite provocative circumstances, and had never felt the same way.

She gritted her teeth and turned away from Callan Storm. She continued holding the flashlight. "I thought you were in a hurry." Even though she stared at the wall in front of her, she felt his eyes on her and kept imagining that rock-hard body.

He didn't reply. Just before she called out again, he plucked the Mini Maglite from her hand.

"Let's go." His warm breath ghosted against the back of her neck and raised goose bumps that tightened her scalp.

When she turned, he'd already moved on. He reached into the closet once more and took out a brown bomber jacket. By the time he reached the door, he'd already shrugged into it and picked up her travel bag.

He nodded to the bed. "Don't forget your makeup case."

Eryn took a step back to the bed and tried to act as if she hadn't forgotten about the case. She had, though, and that irritated her. She was good at keeping up with things, with noticing details. Her job required an attention to detail.

She stepped through the open door and resisted the impulse to look down the hall at the investigation still going on. "Where are we going?"

"Out of the hotel."

"Then what?"

"Then we see if your images help us find a direction. For the moment we need to evade the police dragnet. Take the elevator."

For a moment Eryn started to ask why, then she realized that the police would still be watching the stairwells. Going that way would have been suspicious. She stepped into the elevator alcove.

Luck was with them and they caught one of the cages just as the doors opened. Two couples in evening wear and a boy in his teens playing a portable game system stood inside.

The button for the main floor was already pressed. Eryn watched the levels ping as they dropped.

One of the men spoke up. "Do you know what the fire alarm was about?"

Eryn glanced at the mirrored surface of the elevator door.

Callan didn't speak. She answered for them. "There's a party on our floor."

"That's where the police and the fire departments seemed intent on gathering. I presume there's nothing amiss."

"There's no fire."

The elevator dinged again when they arrived at the second floor. The doors opened to a group of people standing in the alcove. One of the men in the group waved them off. "We'll take the next one."

On the first floor, the doors opened again. Eryn led the way out, surprised to see the crowd that filled the foyer. Evidently not only the guests staying the night had come down from the towers, but the casino had temporarily lost some of its patrons as well. The security people were out in force.

"Let's go." Callan took the lead and headed for the side entrance.

"Wait." Eryn turned away from him and headed back toward the concierge.

The man was absent from his post, but she spied him talking to some of the guests, letting them know that the fire scare had been a false alarm. Nobody was talking much about the shootout in the parking garage. Apparently that news hadn't spread yet.

Eryn stopped at the concierge desk and leafed through the pamphlets in the shelves. A map of the hotel and casino lay in the mix. She pulled it out and consulted it briefly as Callan caught up with her. He was scowling again.

"What are you doing?" He loomed at her side.

"Trying to appear inconspicuous. How's that working for you?"

"We need to get out of here."

"We also need more information if we're going to try to find out who took your future brother-in-law." Eryn located the main desk and headed for the hallway just to the left of it.

"Where are you going?"

"The security office." She avoided Callan's grip, sidestepping and putting a chair between them at the last minute.

Callan quick-stepped and caught up with her. His big hand wrapped around her forearm but he didn't try to stop her. "Why?"

"Because they'll have video footage of everything that happened. I'm going to try to get a copy of it."

"You think you can do that?"

"I know I won't get a copy if I don't try."

Callan's grip fell away and he paced her through the crowded area. He didn't ask her any more questions.

As they passed the check-in area, Eryn gazed at the television in the corner of the room. A small crowd had gathered there to watch the breaking news on the local channels. Video footage of the hotel filled the screen while the neatly groomed male anchor occupied a corner and talked calmly. Script ran across the bottom of the screen.

Fire alarm caused near panic at th—

When Callan caught her arm and tugged, Eryn whipped her head around and just managed to avoid colliding with a heavyset man carrying a poodle. She excused herself but hurried past him into the next hallway. She turned left at the intersection and stopped in front of a metal door—Security/Authorized Personnel Only.

Eryn rang the buzzer and looked up at the fish-eye camera lens mounted above the door.

"Can I help you?" The voice was male, well modulated and slightly anxious.

Eryn took her agency ID from her purse and held it up to the camera. "Can you see this?"

The camera lens flickered. "Sure."

"I need a favor. Professional courtesy."

"We're on lockdown."

"I know. That's why I need the favor. My partner and I were watching over a principle. We lost him in the excitement."

"Not my problem, Ms. McAdams."

"The principle is a high roller. Help me out and I can get you comped at the casino I'm working for. I can get your supervisor comped, too."

For a moment there was no response. "This guy that big?"

"Big." Eryn lied effortlessly. In Vegas everything spun around the casinos and the big money they pulled in. Whales—high rollers that spent a lot at the tables and in the hotels—were an important part of that business. The money trickled through the city, spun through the Strip's veins like a junkie's favorite hit. The story was easily believable. It had happened before.

"I'm not supposed to let anyone in."

"Guy has a jones. If I let him get away without returning him to the hotel, I'm going to lose my job."

Callan stood at her side without saying a word. For a moment Eryn thought she was just going to end up embarrassing herself. She'd been with other security agents who'd used the same bribes to get information on people they were supposed to be keeping up with. Just as she was getting ready to give up, the speaker crackled again.

"Get in, find your guy, then get back out."

"Definitely."

The electronic locking mechanism cycled, thumping and clicking as it opened. Finally, it buzzed.

"Come ahead."

Eryn pushed the door in and followed it.

Chapter 5

Feeling uneasy, Callan stepped into the security command on the woman's heels. He'd filed away her name, McAdams, and the fact that she obviously worked somewhere that would give her access to security agencies.

The interior of the post looked like it was capable of launching a moon shot or a major drone offensive in a war zone. Computers and monitors filled the walls. Camera views of the lobby, the elevators, the parking garage and all through the building's hallways cycled through the screens. On the ops Callan had been involved in, he'd never had access to this kind of hardware.

Two men sat in chairs at a long desk. Computer keyboards and microphones occupied the area in front of them. Both of the men wore holstered pistols and dark uniforms. They were in their mid-to-late twenties, the kind of guys that would draw late shifts. Large cups of coffee sat on the desk. The smell of Chinese takeout lingered in the air and balled-up paper sacks sat in the trash can against one wall.

"I'm Ross Lazlo." The guard jerked a thumb over his shoulder. "This is Marty Wynn."

Wynn never took his eyes from the computer monitors. His hands flicked across the keyboard as he tapped in commands. The guy was dedicated, or maybe picking up the slack because his partner was occupied.

"Thanks for the assist." McAdams approached the man and stuck out her hand.

Lazlo smiled and undressed the woman with his gaze. The obvious sexual interest in the man's eyes irritated Callan for reasons he didn't understand, and he didn't know why McAdams wasn't offended by the attention.

"You're welcome. Can I call you Eryn?"

The woman nodded and Callan tucked that name away as well.

"According to your ID, you're with CyberStealth Security."

"I am."

Callan didn't recognize the name. Since he'd been in Vegas, he'd seen a number of different security agencies. It seemed like everybody in the city had their own private police.

"My partner's gonna check that out, but I think you're okay." Lazlo touched his nose. "I can smell things that aren't right, you know."

Eryn gave a small smile. "Lucky guy. I have to check everything."

"And your guy still got away from you."

"It's hard to guard someone who doesn't want to be guarded."

"I get that. They get what they deserve, I says. But let's see if we can give you a hand. Who's your whale?" Lazlo turned his attention back to the screens.

"I'm not at liberty to say."

"Got a picture?"

"I'll know him when I see him."

"You play things pretty close to the vest there, sister."

"Vegas is that kind of town."

"Why couldn't you keep up with him?"

"There was a lot of confusion at the time."

"Confusion?" Lazlo looked more interested and more concerned. "Did he get caught up in that situation up on the fourth floor?"

"The bachelor party?" Eryn nodded guilelessly. "He knew

somebody there. Got a phone call from someone attending the party. We arranged for a limo to bring him over, then we lost him during the break-in."

Looking more concerned, Lazlo sat up straighter in the chair. He tapped computer keys. "He wasn't the guy taken, was he?"

"I hope not. Can you show me some footage of the party?"

Lazlo shook his head. "No cameras inside the room. Private function. We can't do that. But I got footage of the hallway outside."

"Show me that."

Standing behind the two security men, Callan watched as events suddenly reversed on one of the center computer screens. The view was from outside the room where the party had been held. He recognized the room number.

For a moment dozens of people stood around in the hallway, all gesturing wildly and trying to talk at the same time. Then they rapidly gathered and retreated into the room, walking and running backward.

In the next minute, the men in the black uniforms ran backward up the hall and into the room. The video feed stopped.

Lazlo turned his attention to Eryn. "Did you see your whale?"

"Not in that group."

"Seems like everybody inside that room came out after all the excitement was over."

"The excitement's still not over. I was just up there. And not everyone got out of that room. I talked to a guy still there."

Callan leaned in. "Can you back that up to the time those men first broke into the room?"

Irritation twisted the man's features. "Sure I can."

"Do it."

Lazlo looked as if he was going to refuse on general principle and Callan realized he'd overstepped whatever boundaries Eryn had established. Frustration nipped at Callan. When he gave orders he was used to being obeyed in a heartbeat because lives were on the line.

Daniel's life might be on the line now.

Smiling, Eryn stepped forward and clapped a hand on Lazlo's shoulder. "Please. Back the footage up. My partner's a little edgy. He's new to this."

"Yeah, well, he'd better learn to lighten up if he wants to get anything done. You start throwing weight around this city, you better have the weight to throw." Lazlo glared at Callan.

With her hand still on the man's shoulder, Eryn leaned closer, putting her face next to the security guard's. It was a pure vamp move and Callan knew it. Under the circumstances, her actions were the right play to make, but he still didn't like it. The woman knew what she was doing, and that in itself was worrisome.

"Please."

Rolling his shoulders like a prizefighter, Lazlo nodded. "Sure. For you. A favor. Maybe you can do me a favor some time."

Callan's dislike for the man grew. Eryn had already promised some kind of comp arrangement. Now Lazlo was pushing for more, trying to make it personal. Callan forced his anger away and focused on what he was trying to achieve. Eyes on the prize, soldier.

The problem was Eryn McAdams was distracting. Standing behind her, Callan couldn't help but be aware of her body as she leaned forward to distract Lazlo. Steeling himself and reining in his attention to peripheral matters, Callan watched the screen.

Everything happened in reverse. The men in the dark uniforms ran backward into the room. A short time after that, they walked slowly out of the room. Along the way they holstered their weapons under the loose folds of the coveralls.

"Can you find out where those guys came from?" Eryn pointed at the kidnappers.

"Already tried. Me and Marty searched for them first thing."

Lazlo shrugged. "Guys came out of the elevator in those coveralls."

"What elevator?"

"This one." Lazlo tapped the keyboard in rapid syncopation.

A camera view swelled up and filled the screen with the interior of an elevator cage. The doors opened and an arm thrust in with a spray can clutched in a fist. A moment later a green paint mist occluded the camera lens.

"Guys were smooth." Lazlo cracked his knuckles. "Hit the camera first thing and blinded us. Whoever they were, they probably dressed in the elevator." He pulled up another report. "See? Shows the elevator remained stationary for forty-three seconds. We don't see them again till they stepped off on four. The camera in the elevator and just outside it in the lobby went down about twenty minutes before that."

"You didn't think maybe someone should have checked that out?" Callan couldn't keep the accusation from his tone.

Lazlo turned on him. "Sure we did. We sent a report. It's what we do. We had guys converging on the elevator. They just got there too late. We had to hunt for them. The elevator stopped at every floor and we weren't sure where they got off. Didn't know what was going on, so we were spread thin. Back off, buddy. We know what we're doing here."

Callan held back a scathing retort, but just barely. He wanted to point out they'd just allowed him access to their comm control without even knowing who he was during a high-stakes situation.

"Hey, Ross." Eryn shifted so she was between Lazlo and Callan. "Do you have any footage of the encounter out in the garage?"

Suspicion filled Lazlo's gaze then and took some of the edge off the sexual interest. He was starting to turn wary. "How do you know about that?"

"One of the guys upstairs told me the kidnappers killed someone in the garage."

Lazlo shook his head. "That doesn't have anything to do with your whale. Not unless they took your guy, and you said they didn't do that." He glared at her with increasing suspicion. "You want to tell me what you two are really up to?"

The other guard, Wynn, shifted in his seat and drew Callan's attention. One of the monitors in front of him showed the action in the hallway as Callan dragged Eryn after him in pursuit of the kidnappers. Dressed in the devil costume, Eryn wasn't recognizable, but Callan was.

Wynn's head jerked around as his hand dropped down to his holstered pistol. He pushed up from the chair.

Moving quickly, Callan sidestepped and launched a side kick that caught the guard in the side of the face. Wynn flew backward and his pistol sailed out of his hand. The man was unconscious before he rebounded from the wall. Before the guard slumped to the floor, Callan snagged the pistol from the air.

Spinning, Callan instinctively flicked the safety off the pistol and brought it up before him while Lazlo raised his own sidearm. Inside the small room, their weapons were almost in each other's faces. A split second before he pulled the trigger, Callan remembered the man in front of him wasn't an enemy. Shooting him wasn't an option.

But he was about to be shot.

Panicked, not believing how things had just gone insane inside the control room, Eryn lowered herself and drove a shoulder into Lazlo's meaty side. Adrenaline had fired through her system and her strength was greater than she realized. She managed to lift the man off his feet and knock him back toward his partner. The air went out of him in a loud gasp.

Lazlo's pistol boomed inside the control center and nearly deafened Eryn. She never wanted to hear a gun go off again outside of a gun range. Fear spiked in her and she kept expecting to feel Callan's bullets plow into her back. But she kept her head lowered and bulled into Lazlo, driving him back against the wall and pinning him. Before he could fire again, she jerked the Taser from his equipment belt, rammed it into his leg, broke physical contact with him and triggered the charge just as he started to lunge at her.

Staggered by fifty thousand volts, Lazlo dropped his weapon and sank to the floor. Recovering only slightly, he immediately reached for his pistol. Callan beat him to it.

"Facedown on the floor." Callan's voice thundered in the enclosed space. "Now."

Lazlo complied, moving a little slowly after being his encounter with the Taser.

Eryn stared at the security guard, then at Callan. She couldn't believe what she'd just done, because the job she'd worked and trained for was going down the tubes fast. *Idiot! You're an idiot!* She didn't know if she was talking to herself or to Callan.

But she couldn't have stood by and let Callan get shot, either. Lazlo would have shot Callan without hesitation. Things were moving too fast, spiraling even more out of control. She cursed. This was insane.

"You okay?" Callan touched her shoulder gently.

She resented his concern. She was trained for physical encounters. She wasn't some babe in the woods. Angry at him and at herself for making things so much worse, she slapped his hand away and resisted the urge to jolt him as well. If she hadn't been so taken with him she wouldn't have been stupid enough to get this deeply involved in the situation they faced. Now the train was off the tracks.

"I'm fine. Don't touch me." Lungs burning, she took a deep breath. "He was going to shoot you."

"I know."

"Or you were going to shoot him."

"Not a chance. If I was going to, he would have already been dead. You're fast, but you're not fast enough to have kept me from shooting him if I'd wanted to."

Eryn remembered the fluid way Callan had moved, how

he had knocked the other guard out then scooped the flying pistol out of the air. She'd never seen anyone move so *fast*. He'd chosen not to kill Lazlo. She was sure of that. She took another breath and tried to think.

That decision not to kill Lazlo had made Callan even more vulnerable to the man. It had also made her respect Callan more. Eryn felt certain the security guard wouldn't have hesitated about shooting Callan. Lazlo had pulled the trigger as soon as his finger had found it. Only then did she realize they were all lucky no one had gotten hit by a ricochet.

Calmly, Callan took his captured pistol off full cock and tucked it at his back behind his waistband without even thinking about it. The move was totally automatic. He seemed to stand taller, more certain of himself, and she knew that he'd been somehow incomplete without a weapon in his hand. His attention was focused solely on Eryn. "You're sure you're okay?"

"I'm fine."

Callan studied the walls of the room. "Soundproofed, do you think?"

Eryn took a shuddering breath and forced herself to examine the room. The gunshot was loud, though even a soundproofed room might not keep all of the noise inside. "Yes, but you're not going to be able to keep the sound of that shot from being overheard. Somebody's probably already calling it in."

With cool detachment, Callan studied the monitors. "Doesn't look like anyone's headed back this way. I don't hear anyone checking in on these guys over the radio."

"You will."

"If we do, we'll deal with it then."

"We?" Eryn couldn't believe it. "All of a sudden it's *we?*"

He shifted his attention to her. He wasn't even breathing hard. "Unless you want to walk away from this."

Eryn looked at him so calm and collected and resented him even more in that moment. Her career, maybe her life, was sliding right down the toilet as the clock ticked, and he just stood here looking at her. "This isn't something you can just walk away from. These guys know my name. They know where I work." Even saying that aloud undermined her confidence.

"I forced you to do this. That's all you have to say."

For a moment, Eryn seized on that. Maybe she had an out. It would be her word against Lazlo and his partner that she was coerced. The rationalization would probably work for the assault charges. She would need a good attorney, and her job at CS Sec would more than likely slide right down the tubes.

She met his gaze and shook her head. "I'm not going to do that."

Callan held her gaze, then nodded.

The nod irritated Eryn. She didn't know what he meant by it. If he thought she'd somehow ascended to his level, he could—

"Can you get me a copy of that footage?"

It took Eryn a moment to realize he'd asked her a question, and a moment more to understand what that inquiry was about. "What?"

"The abduction sequence. I need a copy." He hesitated. "We need a copy."

"Why?" Even as she asked that, though, Eryn was already sliding into Lazlo's seat. She'd liked the sound of that *we*.

Callan didn't bother to talk. He knew she was working on the data retrieval. He kept his attention on the monitors. "If we're found out, we'll have to move."

"We haven't done anything wrong." Guiltily, Eryn looked at the unconscious man and Lazlo weakly trying to get to his feet. "Maybe there's a problem with the assault, but these guys overreacted."

"Yeah." Callan looked around the room and focused on a first-aid kit hanging on the wall. "Not really worried about the assault charges." He crossed to the kit and opened it.

"You should be worried. Lawyers here in Vegas are blood-thirsty." Eryn brought up the menus and cycled through them.

"Are you going to be able to make a copy of that footage?"

Callan removed a thick, wide roll of surgical tape from the kit. He also took out a large pressure bandage.

"Yes. No problem. The system is like ones I've trained on."

Returning to Lazlo, Callan gazed down at the man. "Roll over. Onto your stomach."

"What are you going to do?" Lazlo's words were slurred and his eyes weren't tracking correctly. Eryn felt bad about that.

Callan reached down, caught the man by the collar and yanked him up like he would a reluctant child. Then he dropped him onto the floor on his stomach. Before Lazlo could respond, Callan placed a knee in the middle of the man's back and caught one of his arms. The tape shrilled as he unrolled it to bind Lazlo's hands behind his back.

"Hey! Stop! You can't do this!"

While he was talking, Callan shoved the pressure bandage partially into his mouth. Lazlo's words became garbled and much softer. He squealed in fear and outrage. Callan wound more tape around the pressure bandage and the guard's head, making big loops and pulling them tight.

Eryn watched all the action from the corner of her eye, but she stayed at work at the keyboard. She'd located the video file and hoped the time/date stamp was accurate.

"Are you about done?" Callan returned to the computer workstation.

"Yes. I've isolated the minutes we want. Just gotta transfer them. You're talking uncompressed video and audio files. They're big." If she hadn't been in the habit of carrying a large capacity thumb drive on her key ring to transfer video files from her casework, she'd never have had the memory to store what she was taking. As it was, the files made a tight fit on the drive.

Something buzzed in Callan's pocket. He took out his cell and gazed at it. Then he frowned and put the phone away. For the first time that night he looked vulnerable, less certain of himself. Eryn almost felt sorry for him. Callan was a guy used to being in control.

"Problem?"

Callan took a breath. "My sister."

"You're not going to talk to her?"

"No. This isn't the time. I don't have anything for her."

"What are you supposed to have?"

"An idea of where to find Daniel." He frowned and stared relentlessly at the computer screen. His stiff, closed body language told her that any discussion on that topic wasn't going to be tolerated.

The marker showing the download progress moved slowly toward completion, but it was moving.

"Lazlo, I need you to make a connect to the garage team. I can't raise them from where I'm at."

Eryn scanned the monitors, looking for the speaker.

"Here." Callan tapped the second screen in the middle with a forefinger.

On the screen, a man in his late forties stared up expectantly at the camera. A mustache framed his upper lip and he looked tired. "Lazlo?" He peered more intently at the camera.

A frigid chill doused Eryn. She didn't know how close the nearest team was, but she was certain they wouldn't be far. She was only minutes away from getting busted. She forced herself to swallow…and to breathe.

Impatiently, the mustached man pointed at one of the nearby guards. "Hallaway, you're with me." Together, the two men headed out of the room and vanished from the camera's point of view. A moment later, the radio crackled again. "Anybody got eyes on the comm center?"

"We're running out of time." Callan sounded calm.

"I know. There's no way to hurry this up." Frustrated, Eryn watched the download progress. The bar had almost filled.

"Take it. Let's go."

Eryn shook her head. "No."

Callan reached for the thumb drive and she blocked the effort by grabbing his wrist. "Don't. You take that out now, before it has a chance to finish, that video file isn't going to do you any good. It'll fragment and be corrupted. You won't be able to get anything off it except a few scattered artifacts, like pieces of a puzzle."

The corded muscle pressed against her palm held solid for a moment, then relaxed. She knew if he'd wanted to, he could have broken her grip. Of course, then she'd have had to resort to more drastic measures. She hadn't risked her job just to walk away empty-handed. He pulled his arm back and she regretted losing the feel of him.

"I'll stay until it finishes. You go."

"No." Eryn wasn't going to be told what to do. Not by him. Despite the danger she was in, her thoughts lingered on the warmth and strength of his flesh against hers. "You don't know how to eject the thumb drive properly."

"You just unplug it."

She gazed at him and shook her head, wondering where he'd been and how he'd possibly gotten so far out of touch with technology. "No, that's not how you do it. You could get the same fragmentation."

Drawing in a deep breath in disgust, Callan glanced back at the computer monitor and ran a hand through his short-cropped hair.

"If you can't manage a computer, how do you expect to get your future brother-in-law back?" Eryn tapped the keys to safely eject the thumb drive.

"Did those guys back there look like geeks to you?"

Eryn didn't reply. There was no need to. She had no problem remembering how afraid she'd been when the man had grabbed her and talked about taking her with them. The men were hard, dangerous. A lot like Callan. He was right: he was definitely in his element with those men.

But he was going to have to find them before he could do anything. He glanced at his pocket again and she guessed that Jenny was calling her big brother once more. Callan checked the phone and looked unhappy.

Eryn took the thumb drive from the USB port. "We're done here. Let's go." She got up and headed for the door and Callan matched her stride for stride.

Chapter 6

In the hallway, Callan took her by the elbow and pulled her to the right.

Eryn fought back. "What are you doing? The security guys are coming from that direction." She knew that from the map that had hung on the wall and showed all the hotel's hallways.

"I know."

"You *want* them to see us?"

"If we look like we're heading away from the security team when they arrive, they'll assume—" He stopped speaking as the mustached man appeared in the hallway ahead of him. Three security guards flanked him.

Without a word, Callan reached around Eryn and pulled him close to her as if they were a couple. Eryn only thought about resisting, then realized what he was doing. She leaned into him, feeling that rock-hard body moving against her. The contact drove her senses wild and she felt her heart involuntarily speed up. Her breath caught at the back of her throat. She didn't know if that was a result of her proximity to Callan or because of the situation.

The security team stared at them for a long moment as they neared, then focused on the security room. Eryn took a deep breath as the men passed, and the clean scent of Callan went straight to her head. He didn't use a lot of product and the smell was all virile male. She had to make herself pull away from him as they turned the corner.

"What now?" She folded her arms to make sure she didn't reach out to touch him again.

"We're leaving."

"My car is in the parking garage."

"Leave it. Security and the police will be all over the garage."

Mentally chiding herself for not realizing that, Eryn kept moving. "You expect to just walk out of here?"

"I'm not stopping."

From his unflinching tone, Eryn knew he meant it, but there was also a lot of risk. "The guy back there recognized you."

"He was looking at footage while I was standing right next to him."

At the entrance to the main lobby, Eryn spotted a large television spewing live news coverage. Behind the African-American anchor, footage of the bachelor party rolled. It was followed almost immediately by video that had obviously been shot by someone with a camera phone. The new video showed Callan dragging Eryn in her skimpy costume out into the lobby.

Putting a hand on Callan's broad shoulder, Eryn stopped him and nodded at the television. "Everybody's going to be looking watching that footage for the next few minutes."

Callan growled with displeasure. "How did they get that?"

"Everybody's got a camera phone."

"I don't."

"Yeah, you do. I saw your phone." Eryn gazed at him with wonder. "Don't you even know the phone you're carrying?"

"I just got it a few days ago when I got back stateside. My sister wanted a way to get hold of me."

"How did she get hold of you before?"

"She didn't." Callan didn't elaborate and Eryn knew she wasn't going to get any further details.

Spotting a gift shop, Eryn started over for it. "C'mon."

Callan looked like he was going to argue, but she'd already

walked away. And she had the thumb drive. He trailed after her, but the hard set of his face—she watched him in the reflection of the gift's shop's windows—let her know he wasn't happy.

Inside the shop, Eryn walked to one of the walls filled with items designed for tourists—shot glasses, key chains, decks of cards and other items. She selected a baseball cap with I [heart] Las Vegas across the front, then a pair of knockoff sunglasses with amber lenses.

Callan grimaced.

"Buy them. They'll break up the planes of your face. The hat provides an identifier most people will see and never look at you. Think of it as urban camouflage. I'll be okay, most people will only remember my outfit."

Without comment, he took the items to the counter. A young saleswoman with a hard body and daring cleavage turned on a high-wattage smile when Callan stopped in front of her.

"Can I help you with anything? Give you a tour?"

"Thanks, but I'm not going to be in town very long."

The salesclerk flashed him a mock sad smile that didn't look completely false. Eryn wanted to go over and point out that Callan hadn't entered the gift shop alone. She refrained, but she crossed her arms and stared at the younger woman with disapproval.

Without missing a beat, the salesclerk took a card from the counter, flipped it over and scratched a pen across the back hurriedly. When she was finished, she presented the card to Callan. "That's my personal number. In case your plans change. Or if you get a chance for a day trip."

"Sure." Callan took the card, flashed the young woman a smile that the clerk instantly bought into and walked toward the door.

Eryn fell into stride with him. She was concerned about their chances of walking through the lobby unnoticed. Callan wasn't a guy who escaped attention, but she couldn't get her mind off what had just happened. The clerk's nerve of coming on to him even after she'd seen Eryn practically lead him into the shop was annoying. She ground her teeth, trying to figure out why she was taking the disrespect she'd just been shown more personally than she'd taken being shot at and almost abducted. Tonight was the strangest mix of feelings she'd ever experienced.

"What?" Callan spoke without looking at her.

"What?"

"You're upset."

"I'm not upset."

Callan shrugged. His head swiveled smoothly as he watched the pedestrian traffic through the lobby.

Eryn took in a breath and let it out. They were almost to the door, but she couldn't let it go. He was supposed to do something, but she didn't know what it was he was supposed to do. She spoke before she knew she was going to. "I'm not upset."

Brows furrowed, Callan gazed at her.

"About anything."

"Okay."

Eryn tried to keep her mouth shut, but she couldn't. "I just wanted you to know."

"Sure."

Two police officers and two plainclothes detectives cycled through the lobby. Handy-talkers crackled with radio static.

"Keep focused on the door." Callan's voice was a soft whisper in her ear. "Don't look at them. Just think about walking out. We're just two people going to try our luck at other tables."

Eryn swallowed and hated the guilty way she felt. She hadn't done anything wrong, but she felt criminal. That was an unaccustomed feeling for her. She was a straight-arrow person. Good in school, a good friend, a good employee.

Except she'd just assaulted a hotel security guard after gaining access to their headquarters through subterfuge. Every step she took toward the door, she kept expecting one of the police officers to confront her or one of the hotel security staff to arrest her.

Almost miraculously, Callan led her over the threshold and out of the hotel. Immediately, the clamor and artificially chilled air trapped inside the hotel faded away, replaced by the noise of the street and the fetid air of the desert at night. Carbon monoxide burned her nostrils and the back of her throat.

"When we get a cab, we need to go somewhere to regroup." Callan spoke calmly, as though they were out for an evening stroll.

"If you go somewhere public, you're taking a chance on being recognized."

Callan shook his head. The aviator lenses glinted darkly, masking his eyes. "We go somewhere big enough that we get lost in the crowd."

"Where do you plan on watching the video we download?"

Callan's jaw worked. "I don't know this city."

"We can go to my apartment." Eryn regretted the suggestion as soon as she had put it out there. She hoped that Callan would turn her down.

"Okay." He didn't sound happy about it and she didn't know if she should take offense. "Don't give the cab driver your address. Pick someplace public, a café, a convenience store, something like that. Some place nearby. I don't want to leave a trail straight back to you."

"There's already a trail leading to me. My address is on file with the company I work with."

"The people you work with might stall. The front office that has your paperwork should be closed."

"It is." Eryn hadn't even thought about that.

"Then we can be off the grid for a few hours. Your driver's license has your current address. The police can pull that, but it might take them a little while to get around to it. They'll have their hands full with everything going on here. And Daniel's family is going to throw a lot of weight into the middle of this."

"My driver's license doesn't have my current address. Renee

and I moved into a new apartment a few months ago. I haven't gotten the address changed." Eryn hadn't relished waiting in line to get the change done. "I've got to renew my license in another month. I was going to take care of it then."

"Even better. Gives us more time. Will your roommate be home?"

"No. Her son is sick and so is she. She went to her mother's for the evening. That's how I ended up in the cake. I was covering for her."

"Gives us more time. Fewer people involved."

Glancing at Callan, Eryn felt miffed at his casual acceptance that they would be at her apartment alone. She didn't know whether to be worried about being there with him or look forward to it. Then she told herself she was being foolish for even thinking about that.

Thankfully there wasn't a line waiting on the cabs. Police vehicles filled the immediate vicinity, though, and they had to walk to one of the outer booths where a hotel attendant stood waiting.

"Cab, sir?" The attendant was a Hispanic guy in his early twenties.

"Please." Callan gave the guy a couple of folded bills.

The attendant stepped out and waved a white-gloved hand to a waiting cab. The cab pulled up smoothly and the attendant opened the door.

Eryn slid into the cab and Callan dropped in beside her. She asked the driver to take them to a bodega only a couple blocks from her apartment. The car got underway immediately, sliding into the heavy traffic along the Strip.

Twisting in the seat, Eryn glanced back at the hotel, not believing everything that had taken place in the past hour. Neon lights painted the Strip and Vegas seemed more otherworldly than ever.

When she turned back around, she noticed Callan staring at the streets, at the flickering signs and at the cars that filled the street. Beside them, a limousine sped by. Three men in their twenties stood in the opening of the sunroof. Bare chested, they held champagne bottles in their fists and howled at the sky.

Eryn thought she recognized one of the guys from a movie she'd seen recently, but she wasn't certain. Maybe they were just scions of wealthy families. Or maybe they were simply three buddies who had pooled their money together for a few days of vacation to go crazy.

Callan snorted and shook his head.

Eryn cleared her throat. "I take it you disapprove."

He looked at her. "Yeah, I do. I don't see how anyone would want to live in a city like this."

"You get out past the few streets that make up the Strip, you run right into desert. There aren't many places to go outside the city where people can make enough money to live. Maybe you didn't notice that on your way in from the airport."

"I slept."

"Not much of a sightseer?"

Callan was quiet for a moment. "I am when there's something worth looking at."

"What would that be?"

He hesitated. "Forest or jungle or plains. Somewhere green where the world is quiet and you don't see people for miles. There's a place I know where a waterfall plunges from the mountains into the river below. There aren't any roads into that place. You have to hike three days to get there. It's one of the more peaceful areas I know."

"Where is it?"

"The Cape Floral Kingdom."

"Where's that?"

"The Western Cape of South Africa. In the Fynbos eco-region. The climate there is Mediterranean, not tropical." He paused and a small smile lifted the corners of his mouth. "It's beautiful there."

"What were you doing in Africa?"

Neon colors stained Callan's hard face as the cab wove

through the traffic. The soft, colored lights blurred some of the firm lines of his features. "Same as now. Looking for people."

"Saving them?"

"Some of them." The answer was flat and cold. "Others were like the men that took Daniel. Most of those I left where I found them."

The emotionless answer sent a shiver through Eryn, and she wondered who she had climbed into a cab with.

Callan's phone buzzed. He reached into his pocket, took out the device, checked the view screen briefly and put it away.

"You need to talk to her. She's going to be worried."

Callan shook his head. "Daniel's missing. In enemy hands. Talking to me isn't going to help Jenny. She's not going to be happy till Daniel's safe." He put the phone away.

Less than thirty minutes later, the cab wheeled into the convenience store. Callan paid the driver, added a tip and got out. The wind pushed against him and he hated the bright white light that streamed from the small supermarket.

"My apartment is that way." Eryn pointed up the street that ran alongside the bodega.

"Okay, but first we're going to get some things." Callan hated putting off the chase, but he knew they had to make a few purchases. In order to take up the pursuit, they had to be ready.

Instantly suspicious, Eryn studied him. "What things?"

Callan touched her jawline just under a scrape there. "You need to get these scratches and abrasions taken care of before they get infected." He looked at her and couldn't help noticing how kissable her full lips were, then he cursed himself because he had no business noticing something like that. He couldn't shake it, though. The woman was definitely pinging his radar.

"And I need some hair dye. Unless you have some at home."

She looked angry enough to bite his finger off, and only then did he realize that he was still touching her face. "This color is natural."

"Maybe your roommate colors her hair."

"She does sometimes, but I don't think you'd look good in orange, electric-blue or lime-green."

Callan shook his head.

She smiled at him, taunting. "You could pull it off in this town."

Without a word, Callan turned from her and headed into the bodega.

"Do you always growl like that?" She fell into step with him.

"I didn't growl." At least, Callan was pretty sure that he hadn't growled. He wasn't in the habit of growling, but the woman got under his skin in ways he'd never before experienced.

"See? There you go again."

Inside the bodega, Callan moved swiftly. He knew time was working against them. The kidnappers were going to move fast, and he was sure that if Daniel was still alive—he's alive!—he wouldn't last more than a few minutes after the ransom was paid.

He moved through the aisles with Eryn at his side. She was a distraction. He couldn't help but notice the way her pants hugged her ass when she walked ahead of him, or when he turned around to check on her. In some insane way, she seemed even more attractive now than she had in the devil costume, when the red handful of material had strained to cover what little it had covered.

While he shopped, his phone buzzed twice more. Both times it was Jenny. He knew she was worried, about Daniel and about him, and he felt guilty for not calling her. But he wasn't ready to deal with that yet. When he did call her, he was going to need information, and he felt bad about that, but he needed to be able to distance himself from her pain and fear.

"I have food at the apartment."

Callan ignored Eryn's protests and put steaks into the plastic basket he'd gotten at the front of the bodega. "I don't know what you have."

"I could tell you."

"I don't have time to play guessing games with your inventory." Callan headed for the vegetables and picked out some potatoes. "Besides, you have a roommate. What you had this morning might not be there tonight."

"I'm not cooking for you."

"I know how to cook."

"I thought you were in a hurry. Why do you suddenly have time to cook?"

"I was in a hurry to get of the hotel. Gearing up is going to take some time."

"Gearing up?"

Callan ignored her question. He flicked a glance at the older woman standing at the counter with her arms folded. She looked tired and worn, but her focus was on the television against a nearby wall on a shelf. The program was about some kind of ghost hunters. Personally, Callan didn't believe in ghosts, and even if they had existed, they wouldn't have been as frightening as some of the men he'd faced over the years.

"What are you talking about?"

"I need equipment."

That caused her to look down for a moment. Callan kept walking through the aisles, picking up items from his mental shopping list. The meal was going to be simple but filling. Once he got underway, he didn't think—*hoped*—there would be anything to break his stride.

"That's not a good idea."

"Really? You think those guys busted in on the bachelor party, sprayed bullets and they're just going to ignore the fact that they have those weapons?" Callan shook his head. "These guys are already facing serious penalties for kidnapping and for felony homicide. They're not going to give themselves up, and anyone going up against them had better be able to defend himself."

"Do you know how many laws you're planning on breaking?"

"No more than necessary, but I'll break every law I have to in order to get Daniel back." Callan put two boxes of granola bars into his basket. "I've got a friend who can hook me up with what I need. But it's going to take some time. In the meantime, we see what we can learn from the video footage you got."

"The police and FBI might have Daniel back by then."

Callan shrugged. "If they do, it won't hurt my feelings. But I really don't think that's going to happen." He searched through the small hand-tools section. When he found what he was looking for, he plucked it from the shelf.

"Duct tape?" Eryn sounded as if she couldn't believe it. "What are you going to need duct tape for?"

"I don't know. Yet. But it's been my experience that when you need it, you really need it." Satisfied that he'd gotten everything he needed, Callan headed for the front of the store to pay. All told, they hadn't been inside the bodega fifteen minutes.

Chapter 7

Callan carried the groceries and Eryn's travel bag. Eryn carried her makeup case and had offered to help, but he'd refused. From that point on, she ignored the fact that the bags probably got heavy. He walked beside her as if he was an automaton operating on an agenda. He was watchful, though. He never stopped looking around, never dropped his guard for a moment, but he didn't act like he felt threatened. He was totally in control of his surroundings.

She was surprised at how safe she felt with him. Her neighborhood wasn't a bad area. Renee had made certain of that when she'd picked the apartment. But walking alone in the night with the neon glow of the Strip so very near made Eryn feel vulnerable. Walking during the day was different. Nights always seemed filled with danger.

Part of that threatening feeling came with the knowledge of the crimes taking place in the city. Vegas was a twenty-four-hour town. The entertainment and the gambling didn't stop. Neither did the crime. But the darkness at times brought out darker predators. The violence done then wasn't just about money or control. Sometimes it was just about the savagery.

Those cases, many of them against women, had worried Eryn when she thought about what Renee did.

At the apartment building, Eryn slid her key through the security door and they went inside. They took the elevator up to the sixth floor, then walked down to the apartment she shared with Renee and her son. As usual, several of Devin's toys lay scattered around the room. Eryn resisted the impulse to clean up or apologize.

In the awkward silence, Callan stood in the hallway holding the bodega bags and the travel bag.

Eryn gazed at him and lifted an inquisitive eyebrow. "Coming in?"

"Yeah." He stepped inside the room, held the bags in one hand and took the hat off.

The respectful way he conducted himself surprised Eryn. Most men didn't bother to take their hats off inside these days. Her father did, but even he was a throwback to another generation. She wondered if Callan's gesture was just military training, but her intuition was that the behavior that was something ingrained into Callan.

"You're not a vampire, are you?"

Callan blinked at her in annoyance. "What are you talking about?"

"Vampires can't enter someone's home until they're invited. Since I had to invite you in, I thought I'd ask."

"No. I don't like invading someone's personal space."

"Didn't seem to slow you down earlier when you grabbed me."

"I thought you had something to do with Daniel's abduction. The rules were different then."

Rules? Eryn didn't know that if she liked that or not. Guys with rules had a lot of expectations and generally carried a lot of baggage. Then she grinned sourly to herself. She had a lot of rules, too.

He was still talking. "Somebody's personal space is important. You don't really appreciate it until you don't get a lot of it."

"You don't get a lot of personal space? What about that waterfall you were telling me about?"

"I wasn't telling you about the waterfall. I just mentioned it." Callan glanced around the room. "Where's your kitchen?"

Feeling a little put off, Eryn pointed ahead. "On the other side of the dining room wall."

"I'm going to fix a meal for us. Why don't you get cleaned up?" Callan took one long stride forward toward the kitchen.

Eryn wasn't sure if she'd been insulted or not.

"Take the first-aid supplies I bought. If there's something you can't reach, let me know."

No, that wasn't going to happen. For a moment Eryn wondered if he was going to leave while she was in the shower. Then she remembered she still had the thumb drive and he hadn't asked for it.

"You need to dress casual, but something that will stand up to some punishment. Those slacks won't offer much protection. You've got jeans?"

"I know how to dress, Callan."

The three-bedroom apartment came with two complete baths. Renee had been insistent on that. They had to pay extra for the second bathroom, but Eryn had readily agreed. Renee had done that more for Eryn than for herself. Devin was three, and he was a handful and a half. He also loved his bath time. Having two full baths helped keep the peace. Vegas was an expensive place to live and splitting bills between them worked out well.

Eryn went to her closet, selected a pair of jeans, a sturdy pair of boots she could spend hours in and a close-fitting dark red pullover that would keep someone from getting a grip on loose material. She did know how to dress.

Taking the clothing to the bathroom, as well as the thumb drive because she couldn't help thinking Callan might choose that time to double-cross her, she started the shower and stripped. She examined herself in the mirror. Callan had been right about the scrapes and bumps. More of the injuries from the parking garage floor were showing up than she'd expected.

Some of them were tender to the touch, and bruises were already dawning to fruition. She touched the one that Callan had found along her jaw and winced.

"Well, that's going to look wonderful."

Her cell phone on the counter rang and she knew from the tone that it was her boss at CyberStealth. She debated answering.

Paul Giles was one of the senior officers at the security agency and he looked out for her to a degree because he had daughters of his own. In his sixties, Paul was an old-school security agent.

She also liked Paul because he'd stood up for her a few times since she'd been hired by the company. Paul had a tendency to be overly protective in a good way, which also undermined her career there to an extent. In order to succeed, she needed to fight her own battles, but the network at CyberStealth wasn't geared to let a woman do that.

The phone rang again.

In the end, she thought it would be best to know what the agency was planning on doing regarding her confrontation with the hotel security. She scooped the phone up and answered, leaning a hip against the counter. She tried not to feel uncomfortable standing there nude while talking to Paul. He would have died if he'd known. Feeling foolish, she grabbed a towel and wrapped it around herself before answering. "Hello."

"Hey, kid, how are you?"

Eryn took that as a good sign. If Paul had addressed her by her surname, she'd have known he was unhappy. "I'm all right."

"Arthur called me just a few minutes ago and asked me if I'd get in touch with you. So I am."

Arthur Briggs was the main executive, the firstborn son of the owner of CyberStealth. Arthur had Daddy issues and wanted to prove he was better than his old man. As a result, Arthur ran the Vegas office as a harsh taskmaster. The agency's image meant a lot to him.

"Arthur was called by the security chief at Hanover Security. They're saying you broke into their office and took some files. Naturally, Arthur is concerned. And, frankly, so am I."

Eryn grimaced. It hadn't taken Lazlo long to rat her out to his superiors. "I can explain that."

"You can explain zapping a guy with his own Taser?"

"Yes."

Paul chuckled easily. "Must be a great story, kid. Arthur wants you to come in and tell it so he can start doing damage control before the news hits the press."

Eryn paused, knowing this wasn't going to go well. "I can't."

"You can't?"

"Not right now."

Paul's voice deepened and his displeasure rang clear as a bell. "This had better be good."

"The guy I'm with—"

"You're still with the guy who busted up those two guards?" Paul sounded surprised.

The fact that Callan was being credited for taking out both security guards got under Eryn's skin. She supposed Arthur and his cronies would simply think she'd jolted Lazlo while Callan was holding him down. She shelved the anger and pushed it away. "Yes."

"Where are you?" Paul's tone was casual, but the interest was sharp in his words.

Eryn considered her options and knew there was no way to finesse this. "I don't feel comfortable answering that at this time." She hoped fiercely that she was right in thinking that no one at CyberStealth had her new address. The GPS locator on her phone was turned off at the moment, so they'd have a hard time tracing the phone as well.

"Arthur sent a couple agents to your old address. It appears you don't live there anymore."

That surprised her for just a moment, then she realized how adamant Arthur Briggs was about his company's image. The effort to find her, then have Paul call her instead of calling her himself, also showed her how determined the man was to talk to her. Though Paul might have remembered her mentioning moving in with Renee, she hadn't given him the new address. "No."

Silence hissed on the line for a few seconds. Then Paul's voice softened. "Tell me what you've gotten yourself into, kid."

"The guy I'm with—"

"Callan Storm."

Shocked that Paul already knew that, Eryn continued. "He's the future brother-in-law of the man who was kidnapped tonight."

"I see that. We've already got a file started on him. Did you know police are now concerned that he's part of the abduction?"

"Callan didn't have anything to do with that."

"The police don't seem to be as sure of that as you apparently are."

"Then they're already screwing up the investigation." Just like Callan had said they would. The police were looking at the wrong guy. "Callan would have prevented them from taking his sister's fiancé if he could have. The men who took Daniel Steadman knew about Callan. They put a guard on him. I thought he was going to get shot. Ask the other people that were in that room."

"How do you know what happened in that room?" Paul's words were soft, but they were sheathed steel. He was one of the agency's best interrogators.

Too late, Eryn saw that she'd outfoxed herself. Knowing there was no way around it, she owned up to the truth. "Because I was there." Part of the truth, anyway. She went on to explain some more of the details. But Paul wasn't buying Callan's intentions.

"Callan Storm needs to come in and answer their questions."

"He's not going to come in, Paul. He promised his sister that he'd look after her fiancé. He intends to find him and bring him back." As she said that, she remembered the conviction Callan had put into the words. No matter what else she thought of him, and she was confused about that, she knew Callan didn't make promises lightly.

"Then that's his problem. You need to report in so we can clean up the agency's involvement in this matter."

"Callan doesn't know the city."

"That's not your problem."

Eryn gripped her phone more tightly and forced herself to relax enough to speak calmly. Her life, her world, was falling apart and to try to stop that, she'd have to turn her back on Callan. The thought of leaving him out there alone was unappealing.

"It's not my problem, but I am going to help him try to find Daniel Steadman."

Paul blew out a long breath. "Kid, I gotta tell you, you're making a mistake here. A big mistake."

"I got into security to make a difference, Paul. I wanted to help people. Not just put in hours and draw a paycheck. Not just hobnob with casino royalty." Eryn paused, already fearful that she'd said too much. "I thought that was something you could understand."

For a long moment, Paul was silent. Eryn considered hanging up. Paul was heavily invested in the company. His stock portfolio, his retirement, all of that was wrapped up into one little package dependent on CyberStealth. He'd told her that more than once while pointing out how good the agency was to work for. During those times he'd been encouraging her to stick it out and put up with the crap the other agents dished out.

"You know, kid, you're right. And when you're right, you're right. But I gotta tell you something about this guy Callan Storm."

Not believing what she was hearing, Eryn's spirits lifted a little. Maybe there was light at the end of the tunnel after all.

"As soon as we got wind of your involvement in this, we did some background checks. All internet stuff the geek dicks pick up with a single mouse click these days. Daniel Steadman was easy. Scion of a pharmaceutical dynasty in Texas. Callan Storm is a bird of a different feather."

The seriousness in Paul's tone startled Eryn.

"You want my opinion, this guy's a bagful of snakes. His parents were killed when he was sixteen. Nobody else stepped up to take care of him and his little sister."

"Jenny."

"Yeah. She was ten years old. He entered foster care and stayed in till he was eighteen. After that, Storm joined the Marines and started saving money for Jenny. When she turned eighteen, she had college waiting on her and her brother paid her way."

"Not many guys would do that."

"I know. Sounds like a storybook tale, don't it? But while the sister was attending college and getting a degree in pharmacy school where she met Daniel Steadman, Storm ended up in Special Forces and went off the grid. For the past six years, his history is a sucking black hole of no information."

"What does that mean?"

"It means that he's been operating off the books on black ops missions." Paul sounded worried now. "I've seen guys like Callan Storm before, kid. They can look like they've got it together, that they're handling everything, but that's often a lie. These guys aren't part of the civilized world anymore. They don't trust other people, and if they get confused or hurt, they sometimes lash out. People around them tend to get hurt. That guy you're *helping* is a walking time bomb."

For a moment, Eryn stood there feeling stunned. In the back of her mind somewhere she thought maybe she'd had an inkling of what Callan Storm was, but she hadn't known. Not for certain.

"Is she coming in?" Arthur Briggs must have been listening all along.

Paul spoke next. "Kid, it's your call."

"No!" Arthur's voice rose to a near-scream. "No, it's not her call! Get her in here! "

Closing her eyes, Eryn told herself it was time to cut loose. She could simply give Callan the thumb drive, get him out her door and wish him good luck.

Except that he didn't know Las Vegas like she did. He would be more vulnerable and his chances of getting Daniel Steadman back alive—if that was still possible—immediately dropped. She told herself that the police and FBI could handle the kidnapping, but she felt the same way Callan did: those people were going to take too long, move too slow.

The ransom demand would come through soon, if it hadn't already. Once the demands were met, or not met, Daniel Steadman would be dead. The Steadman family would put pressure on law enforcement to find the people responsible for the kidnapping, and if that didn't work, they'd hire private entities like CyberStealth. The kidnappers couldn't be sure that Daniel wouldn't have learned something about them that would work to their detriment while he was with them.

Even as she was thinking about that, working through the logic in her mind, she thought about Megan again. People had known Megan needed help, but no one had lifted a finger. For a moment Eryn remembered what it had been like to walk through Megan's blood, not realizing it till it was too late. Both of them had been fourteen at the time.

Shuddering, she closed off the memory.

"Kid, you still there?" Paul spoke softly this time.

"Yes." Eryn knew her voice was strained. She felt the tightness in her throat. "I'm not coming back in. Not till this thing is finished."

"Sure. I understand."

"What?" Arthur Briggs was almost shouting in the background.

Paul spoke calmly and rationally. "She's not coming in, Arthur. She's got things to do."

"Things to do?" Arthur cursed. "McAdams, you get into this office now. Right now!"

"Good luck, kid. If I can help you in some way, if you think you're getting in over your head, gimme a call on my private line. I don't think Arthur's going to let me take your calls."

Despite the tension of the moment and the tears from the old horror lurking unshed behind her lids, Eryn couldn't help smiling at Paul's quiet aplomb. "Thanks."

"You're welcome. You just take care of yourself, kid. I want you back in one piece."

The broken connection buzzed in Eryn's ear. The phone started ringing again almost immediately. This time the agency number showed in the view screen. She ignored the call and stepped into the hot water of the shower.

A bagful of snakes.

As she stood under the hot needle-spray, Eryn knew she would have never thought of Callan Storm that way. Stubborn, obstinate and infuriating. Those would have been definite things she would have sworn to.

Except he was out there running into machine gun fire trying to get his sister's fiancé back. That was impressive and stupid and maybe even endearing.

A bagful of snakes.

She couldn't help wondering if Paul was right in his assessment. Over the two years she'd worked with Paul, she'd learned to respect his judgment of other people.

Eryn shoved her face under the spray and felt the sting of shampoo in the scrapes and cuts. The pain was slight, but it brought with it a sharper awareness. With her eyes closed, she thought of Callan Storm, how he'd looked, how he'd moved and she reached out to turn the water to a colder degree. Thinking about the man was way too easy and way too welcome.

Chapter 8

Standing bare chested in the kitchen, his shirt hung over one of the bar stools at the breakfast nook, Callan used a meat fork to turn the steaks. He'd been surprised to find an old-fashioned frying pan with raised ridges to keep the meat out of the grease.

The meal was going to be protein and carb heavy, meat and potatoes. He'd baked four potatoes in the microwave and they were cooling now.

His phone and the Glock 20 pistol he'd taken from the security guard lay on the kitchen counter behind him next to a small television. When he'd first seen the television, he'd felt it was wasteful. Now, able to watch breaking local news coverage of Daniel's kidnapping, he understood why the television was there.

So far, there weren't any new angles on the kidnapping. The van the assailants had used had been found only a few blocks away from the hotel. They hadn't wasted any time getting rid of the stolen vehicle. The LVPD and FBI had taken possession for crime scene analysts to inspect, but even if there was something there, the information would come in too late to help Daniel. Callan was certain of that.

The stolen vehicle was merely another lead that deflected law enforcement personnel. He and Eryn needed to work on discovering who the kidnappers were, keep the pressure on them instead of following the script the police and FBI were going to cycle through.

That kind of investigation was good for regular police work, for finding out who had committed a crime where death had already occurred and no one was at risk. A hostage situation required a more aggressive approach.

The most irritating thing developing was the focus on finding Callan himself. His driver's license picture—only a few weeks old because he'd renewed it shortly before flying into the States—appeared often. The reporters had stated that Callan was a *person of interest,* but the overall feeling was that he'd somehow been connected to the abduction.

Callan sipped from a bottle of water he'd purchased at the bodega as he watched the meat. His stomach growled in anticipation of the meal. The earlier dinner had been expensive and gaudy, not something that had filled him up. But even while he watched the food, in his mind he kept playing back the events of Daniel's abduction.

The men who had taken Daniel had inside information. Callan was convinced of that. He'd been involved in too many kidnappings, on both sides. Someone taken that quickly, that cleanly, required inside assistance. The list of people who knew about the bachelor party was huge.

He turned the meat again, wondering if Eryn was going to reappear anytime soon. Before he knew what he was doing, he was imagining her in the shower, water dappling that smooth skin, hair wet and pulled back from her face. She was beautiful, but he got the impression she didn't know that.

He was so lost in the imagined shower sequence that when his phone vibrated and jumped on the counter the movement startled him. He checked the view screen, dreading another call from Jenny. He knew he couldn't put her off much longer, and figured he'd already pushed himself away too much already.

This one wasn't from his sister, though. It showed up as a local number in Las Vegas, which surprised him because he didn't know anyone in the city other than his sister. Then he noticed the name: APE R. SON.

A PERSON.

Callan smiled. This was someone he knew, and he'd been waiting for the return call. As soon as Eryn had left him alone, he'd called Koenig. The German surname roughly translated to "king," and it definitely wasn't Koenig's real name.

Koenig was an enigma. Despite being an asset contracted by the CIA handlers that Callan worked with on his black ops missions, Koenig maintained a veil of mystery. Of medium height and dapper, Koenig wore a goatee and his hair long. There might have been German ancestry in Koenig's family tree, but that wasn't all. On occasion, Koenig could pass for Middle Eastern, Hispanic or Asian. He wore glasses, which made him look bookish and harmless—one of the last things Koenig was. He was one of the deadliest, most cold-blooded men Callan knew.

"Hey, dude." His voice was soft and pleasant, well modulated.

"Koenig. Thanks for calling back."

"Always for you, dude. You know that."

Callan had called one of the drop numbers Koenig had given him for emergencies. In all the years they'd known each other, Callan had never called.

During the ops he'd been assigned to, Callan had gotten to know Koenig. They'd even met for a beer now and again in whatever backwater country they'd been in while between assignments, but that was always pre- or post-mission. Not any kind of social thing. Callan didn't do social obligations. He didn't know what Koenig did, and he didn't ask, but the man had never casually contacted him. Koenig was as close to a friend as Callan had, primarily because they had a history and respected each other's privacy.

"Your call came in as a local number. You're not in Vegas, are you?"

"No way. I like sure bets. You won't catch me around a

casino. Except at a blackjack table. I can count cards with the best of them, but casinos have people who look for guys like me. I just masked the number in case somebody grabs your cell. Somebody checks it out, it'll lead to a dentist's office."

That was how Koenig worked, always one step ahead.

Satisfied the steaks were done, Callan took them out of the frying pan and placed them on a plate. The smell of cooked meat was wonderful and he was hungry, but he had no real appetite. Not with Daniel out there and Jenny not knowing what was going to happen to the man she loved. "I've got a situation."

"Figured you did, dude. Not like you to make social calls. I consider that one of your redeeming qualities. We're busy people."

Despite their acquaintanceship, Callan didn't know everything Koenig did. The CIA used Koenig for aggressive ops, assassinations and asset destruction, but where he was most dangerous was behind a computer. The man could hack and subvert anything that connected to the internet. Callan was also convinced that he didn't want to know everything Koenig did, but when the man said he would do something, he did it, no matter how bloody or how dangerous.

"My sister's fiancé got kidnapped. I'm trying to find him. If I'm going to do that, I'm going to need help."

"Dude, I didn't know you had a sister."

Callan hadn't mentioned Jenny. He kept her away from his work. When he was in the field, he left behind everything that would tie him to her, including any stories. As best as he could, he'd made her safe from his world. "I do. Her name is—"

"Jenny. Yeah, I know, dude. I was just kidding about not knowing you had a sister. I mean, you've never mentioned her, and no one else with the unit has, either. She's listed as your beneficiary and you've been sending part of your income to a college down in Texas she's been going to. She graduated with her master's this year and she's on board for her doctorate. Congratulations."

Callan didn't say anything, but his gut clenched and he felt angry with Koenig instantly.

"What? You didn't think I'd check you out? Dude, don't take it personal. I peek into the files of everybody I work with. I'm not going to let somebody I don't know hang me out to dry. I'm a big believer in revenge. I like to know where to find people who let me down. Or shove a pistol into my face and don't manage to kill me. That's just how I roll."

Forcing himself to relax, Callan reminded himself that Koenig had never mentioned Jenny, either. He'd kept his own counsel and respected Callan's privacy—to a degree.

"The fiancé's name is—"

"Daniel Steadman. Yeah, dude, I got that." The sound of tapping keyboard keys carried over the phone connection. "Hacked into your sister's Facebook account and saw that. Looks like a real storybook romance. Hand-holding and calf eyes. Truly, I thought I was gonna gag."

"What's a Facebook account?"

Koenig sighed. "Dude, you have got to get out of the Third World more and enter the twenty-first century. Facebook is only the biggest invention in social media since the telephone."

Taking the new knowledge into account, Callan worked it around in his mind. "Can anybody hack into someone's Facebook account?"

"Sure. If they know what they're doing. But getting around the security isn't all that hard, dude. Sometimes all you gotta be is just a friend of a friend."

"Can you look at her Facebook now?"

"Sure. Gimme a sec." Only a moment passed. "I'm there. What am I looking for?"

"Did Jenny mention the bachelor party tonight? Where it was? When?"

"Yeah. Even has pics of the hotel. You're thinking the abduction was an inside job."

"It was."

"Got a lot of information here on Facebook, dude. I could

take what I see here, roll into the party, take her fiancé and a half-dozen other guys from rich families. This is like a who's who of please-come-kidnap-me-for-millions list." Koenig cleared his throat. "Probably shouldn't have said that. Kinda disrespectful given your sister's situation."

Callan ignored the callous statements. That was just Koenig's way. He thought aloud when he wanted to get his point across, and he often came out unfiltered. "This was an inside job."

"What makes you so sure? This information is out there for anyone canny enough to get by a little web security. As much money as the Steadman family is worth, a lot of people might be interested in scoring a quick payday."

"The guys in there tonight? They knew about me. They knew I was a soldier. They put a man on me."

"You're more than a soldier, dude. Calling you a soldier is like saying Popeye likes spinach. If they'd known what you really are, they'd have put a bullet through your head and I'd have been short one friend." Koenig cleared his throat. "But you're right, Jenny didn't mention you were a soldier on her Facebook account. I take it you didn't send her any pics of you in the field."

"No. I never sent Jenny any pictures of me on the job in any of the places I've been."

"Okay, so someone's been talking out of school. What do you need me to do?"

"You have time?"

"I keep a full dance card, dude, but I'll always make time for you."

"I don't know how to thank you."

"Buy me a beer next time you see me. Let's get to it. Every kidnapping ends up against the clock. Tick, tick."

"I've got a video of the kidnappers in action. The images are grainy, not at their best. I need you to look at them, see if you can clean them up, then run them through facial recognition software. I want to know who these guys are."

"I'm on it. I'll text you with the website you can upload the
video to. What kind of connection do you have on your computer?"

"I don't have a computer, but the woman I'm with probably
has one."

"Woman?"

"Eryn McAdams. She's an employee of CyberStealth Security Agency."

"Private eye, huh?"

"I don't know."

"No prob, dude. I'll check her out." Koenig let out a low
whistle. "Hey, she's hot. How friendly are you with this babe?
You should probably get *very* friendly. *I'd* get friendly with
her."

Callan immediately felt uncomfortable. "This is business.
She knows the city. I didn't want her involved, but I need an
asset inside the zone."

"Right. Well, she's a great-looking asset."

"Don't tell me she has a Facebook account."

"She does, dude, but she plays it down. From the looks of it,
mostly just family stuff, and not much of that. Mother. Father.
Couple high school and college friends she's kept in touch
with. Her corporate pic at the agency could use some work.
Not very inviting. But this Christmas pic, dude, it's smoking.
Now that's a Mrs. Claus I'd like to see."

Callan washed the frying pan, dried it as best he could and
set it on the stovetop to air-dry. Iron frying pans couldn't be
left wet or they would rust. Living out in the brush as he had
for so many years, he'd developed a habit of taking care of his
equipment.

"What about the file upload?"

"If she's got a desktop at home or a notebook computer,
that's not going to handle what we need done. Uploading
through a regular internet connection would take hours. You
don't have hours."

"No. She downloaded it from the security office in a coupl[e] minutes."

"Different kind of connection. A USB port, that's gonn[a] move data pretty fast. But a regular internet connection? N[o] way. You need to get that data to a T1 connection and uploa[d] it to me."

"Where am I gonna find that?"

"You're in the U.S. of A., dude. Go down to the nearest in[-]ternet café. They'll hook you up."

"I'll go find one."

"Take a breath. Eat dinner with that beautiful lady. It'[s] gonna take me about forty-five minutes to borrow some sat[-]ellite time for us to complete this."

Callan looked at his phone and remembered how Eryn ha[d] told him the unit had a built-in camera. "Can you see me?"

Koenig snorted. "No, dude. You are paranoid. I heard yo[u] doing the dishes. I know when you cook, you do the dishe[s.] Didn't figure you'd popped into her apartment to do her dishe[s.] And yes, I know you're in her apartment. Unless you broke int[o] someone else's apartment. I pinged you on a satellite traceback[.] I can now follow your phone wherever you go. I am that goo[d.] Touch me, dude, I am magic."

Listening to the bravado in Koenig's voice, knowing tha[t] the other man was putting on a show for him to build confi[-]dence, Callan relaxed a little. But he was still afraid for Jenn[y.] He didn't want to fail her.

"We're going to get your future brother-in-law back, dud[e.] Trust me on this. The guys who took him aren't going to d[o] anything to him until they get paid. They can't afford to l[et] this go now. They've gone too far. Somebody's gonna sta[y] greedy. As long as they figure they have a shot at pulling th[is] off, Daniel is going to stay alive and whole. You know tha[t.] It's how we would do it."

Leaning a hip back against the kitchen counter, Callan gaze[d] at the news channel. The neon glow of the Strip floated at th[e]

dges of the camera's view. "I got dead time on my hands till
ou get back to me."

"And you suck at dead time."

"Yeah."

"Talk to your sister, dude. Pick her brain. Make a contact
ree. Who's who. Who's in. Who's out. You know the drill. I
on't have to tell you this."

Embarrassed, Callan hesitated before answering.

Koenig let out a long breath of exasperation. "Dude, you
aven't called her?"

"There hasn't been any time."

A scathing curse erupted over the phone. "I've seen you
harge into rooms filled with bad guys. Now you're a gutless
onder?"

"I don't know what to say."

"She doesn't expect you to know what to say. She just wants
 hear from you. Call her, dude."

"I will."

"In the meantime, we need names of everyone at the party.
ll start with people I see on Facebook. You were there, right?"

"Yeah."

"Anybody suspicious stand out to you? Guy over in the
orner rubbing his hands together in a maniacal way?"

"No."

Koenig heaved a fake sigh. "Hate when there aren't any
bvious clues. Makes it tougher. Got a few dozen guys to go
arough here. Gonna take some time to work up backgrounds,
nancials, on these people. This is about money, probably, so
e're looking for someone who needs a big infusion of cash
ey can't get from legitimate sources."

"I know. But weed out the list. I need results quick."

"Dude, no one's faster than me when it comes to this. Let
e get on it. We'll match up our lists, make sure we didn't
iss anybody. I'll text you with a web address you can upload
at video file to when I have it set up. Is the girl detective any
etter with tech than you are?"

"She got the file from the security guys."

"All right."

"One other thing."

"What?"

"I need ordnance and a clean car. Can you set me up with someone?"

"Does a bear crap in the woods?" Koenig snorted. "You're in Vegas, bro. Wonderland for domestic arms dealers. What do you need?"

"Close in stuff. This is urban. I want to keep things small."

"You got it. And, dude? Call your sister."

The phone clicked dead in Callan's ear. Regretfully, he punched up the address book and looked at Jenny's number. His thumb hovered over the call button.

"Do you always get naked to cook dinner?"

Startled, Callan looked up and saw Eryn standing in the doorway. She looked a lot different in jeans and the pullover. Her hair fell in rebellious ringlets to her shoulders. Even where he was standing, Callan smelled the clean, fresh scent of soap and shampoo and his sexual senses lurched online.

For a moment, he couldn't speak. "It's the shirt."

"You don't like the shirt?" She looked confused.

"I left it in the dining room."

"I know. I saw it on the way in." She folded her arms and her breasts bunched up and looked bigger. "That doesn't explain why you took it off."

Callan had trouble keeping eye contact and his mind wasn't working at peak performance. "The shirt's made out of cotton."

She lifted an eyebrow.

"Cotton soaks up odors. If I'd stood over the stove and cooked the steaks, the meat smell would have seeped into the material."

"Worried about not being fresh as a daisy?"

"Cooked steak isn't something you smell everywhere we're going to be going tonight. The guys we're tracking might notice a smell that's out of place. If I'm coming up behind them and need to be quiet, that scent might give me away."

"Seriously? You think those guys would notice you smelled like a steak?"

"I would notice. When you're out hunting, you need to smell like the environment. Not too much cologne. Not too much soap. It's okay to be clean—"

"Thankful for small favors."

"—but you can't smell like a flower shop or a soap factory." Callan thought she might laugh at him then, or at least shoot him a disparaging glance and think he was borderline insane. "Gives you away every time."

But she didn't. Instead, she nodded, and her eyes tracked down over his body. The curiosity—and maybe something else in her direct gaze—made him feel uncomfortable. "The food's ready." He picked the plates up from the counter and carried them toward the dining area. As he passed her, he felt her breath featherlight and warm against his bare skin. Just for a moment, he thought about turning into her and kissing her, wondering how she'd react to that. You could tell a lot about a person when you kissed them the first time.

If she met the kiss, it could mean she was willing to do whatever it took to stay in his good graces so she could trail along. That could mean she was in on everything, just like he'd thought from the beginning.

He made himself remember how she'd taken him down when they'd faced the gunfire. And he kept moving. Given her innocence in the matter and her desire to help, trying to kiss her would only complicate matters or turn her away from him.

For the moment, although he didn't want to, he needed her.

Chapter 9

Eryn stepped back from the doorway and let Callan pass, but only inches remained between them. Her pulse elevated as she watched the smooth roll of musculature play under his bronzed skin. Judging from her physical reaction to his presence, the cold shower hadn't helped. She grew irritated with him. If he hadn't invaded her home, she wouldn't have to deal with any of this.

The scars stood out against his lean, taut body. Some of them were still pink, and were from recent injuries. Others had turned gray with age. Most were smooth and showed signs of a doctor's care, but others were puckered and had proud flesh where the scar had risen up and stood out against his body.

Although she wasn't a medical expert by any stretch of the imagination, Eryn thought she recognized some of the wounds. She'd had to learn about scars while researching people for clients. Getting rid of a scar was costly. Hair color could be changed with dye, and eyes could be altered with contact lens, but scars tended to stay with an individual. Most of the scars were from gunshots. She counted eight of those, three of them close up because stippling—embedded gun powder tattoos—showed around them, but there were scars from knives and fire as well. The burn scarring stood out on his body like melted wax.

At the table, Callan placed the heavily laden plates near the center. Plates and silverware had already been laid out.

He looked up at her, then hooked his shirt from the back of a chair and pulled it on. He buttoned it rapidly, looking as though he felt foolish for letting her attention bother him. "You look good."

Arms still crossed as she watched him, regretting his decision to put the shirt on, Eryn wondered what he meant by the comment. "Thanks."

"Feel better?"

Reluctantly, Eryn nodded. She did feel better, even if she'd had to take a colder shower than she'd planned. However, she didn't feel generous about letting him know he'd been right.

"Are you hungry?"

The smell of the steak was delectable, and she was surprised at her hunger despite the evening's events. "Yes."

Callan pulled out a seat. "Good." He waved her into the chair.

She sat, knew she wanted to say something, to rebel in some way, but she didn't know what she wanted to say.

Quietly, Callan sat across from her and pushed the plate of steaks toward her. "Not exactly a balanced meal, but we're going to need the extra calories tonight. Once we start moving, we're not going to stop until this is finished. One way or the other."

Eryn took one of the steaks and a potato. After she split the potato, she filled it with butter and sour cream.

After she had her plate, Callan addressed his own meal. He moved with grim determination, expertly slicing the steak into bite-size pieces. He ate with gusto and with total focus, like eating was a chore he had to mark off a to-do list. He used the remote control to switch the television on but muted the noise. He watched the news.

Eryn picked up her fork. "It's hard to believe we're sitting here eating when your sister's fiancé has been kidnapped and the police and FBI are looking for you."

"This is downtime. There's nothing else I can do at the moment. You eat and sleep when you can while you're waiting. That's all you can do."

The soldier mentality irked Eryn. He wasn't just a soldier on a mission tonight. His sister was involved. "What about the video footage?"

"I contacted a guy I know. He's going to look at the footage, enhance it and get back to us. We've looked at it. We'll look at it again, but we're stuck. We need to eat to keep going."

"You called a guy? What guy?"

Callan shifted his attention to her. "A guy I trust. He's good with this sort of thing. In the meantime, you and I are going to work on putting a list together of the people at the party."

"Does this guy have a name?"

"Sure. Everybody has a name." Callan forked up another piece of steak. "He's pulling names from Jenny's Facebook account. People that were listed who were expected to be at the party. We can do the same thing."

"Why can't we send the video to this guy now?"

"Because he has to set up a website we can send it to."

"If I send it from my computer—"

"It'll take hours. I know. He said you might know where there's an internet café with a T1 connection."

Eryn fixed him with her gaze. "I suppose this guy is one of your CIA buddies."

Callan looked at her, put his fork down and blotted his lips with one of the paper napkins that had been on the table.

"You weren't the only one making phone calls." Eryn took a bite of her steak and almost smiled at the annoyance that showed in Callan's sudden stiff posture. He'd been playing Bobby Flay after sending her to scrub up like some child.

Sitting there watching him, Eryn hated the way he could so coldly turn off his interest. He wasn't showing any signs of stress over his sister, over Daniel Steadman, being hunted by the police or the fact that he'd probably cost her the job she'd fought so hard to get.

Silently, she turned her attention to the muted television. Footage of the kidnapping continued to roll. The scene quickly shifted back to the anchor at the desk. Behind her, the words *Ransom Demand* lit up over a picture of Daniel Steadman.

She glanced at Callan, who was already picking up the television remote from the table. He punched the mute button and the audio came on.

"—tell us about the ransom demand the Steadman family has been given, Jess?"

Beside the anchor, a window opened up on a young Hispanic male reporter standing on the street in front of the hotel where Daniel Steadman had gone missing.

Callan cursed and muted the television again. Beside him, his cell phone vibrated on the table. Although she couldn't see the number, Eryn did see a picture pop up on the view screen. The image was that of a young blonde woman in her mid twenties.

"Jenny?"

Callan nodded.

"Have you talked to her?"

His silence answered her, and it took some of the edge off the frustration she was feeling toward him. Both of them had been caught up in circumstances beyond their control.

"Talk to her, Callan. You're the only family she's got. Especially with Daniel gone."

Reluctantly, Callan picked up the phone, got up and let himself out onto the balcony.

Eryn turned her attention back to the television. As she watched the footage roll again, she thought about Callan's "friend" and about the video they'd be uploading to him. Then an idea occurred to her.

Walking back to her bedroom, she took her notebook computer from her desk and returned to the table. She opened the computer and took out the thumb drive. A moment later, she was sorting through the video feed, freezing the stream and taking pictures of the kidnappers. With the current resolution of the video quality, she couldn't see much.

Whoever Callan's friend was, the man was going to need to be a miracle worker to pull anything usable off the footage.

Glancing at the balcony, she studied Callan standing out in the open. The neon gleam of the Strip dawned just beyond him. At first, she couldn't tell anything from his body language. He seemed as implacable as ever. Then he put one hand on the balcony railing and leaned on it for support. Talking to his sister was hard and Eryn felt guilty about badgering him into it.

Feeling even more guilty for watching Callan's discomfort, Eryn picked up his plate and put it in the microwave in the kitchen to keep. Then she forced her attention to the video and looked for another potential image she could capture.

"Callan?"

"Yeah, sis." Callan suddenly felt like the weight of the world had dropped onto him. From the time their parents had died, he'd worried about Jenny. He'd hated signing up for the military when he had, but that was the only place he knew an eighteen-year-old could go to work and earn enough to help take care of a sibling.

During these last years, he hadn't gotten to see Jenny as much as he'd wanted to. There were occasional downtimes between missions, but some of those had been forced because of injuries and he hadn't wanted her to see him then. He hadn't wanted her to worry.

But she had. He'd known that in her letters, in the phone calls they'd shared. She'd thought of him always, and never without worry. That hadn't been what he'd wanted for her.

"Where are you?"

"Safe." That was what he always told her, even when it was a lie. That was the only falsehood he'd learned to effortlessly tell, and it was the only one he'd ever told her.

Her voice broke and it took her a moment to continue. Callan swallowed the lump at the back of his throat. "They said you were there when Daniel was taken."

"I was, but I couldn't get to them. They got away. But I tried, Jenny."

"I know you did. There was nothing you could do." She paused. "Was Daniel all right? The last time you saw him?"

"He was fine. Scared. But he was holding it together." Callan took a breath and distanced himself from the fear and hurt and anger in Jenny's voice. The military had taught him to do that, but they'd never taught him a way to do that easily.

"I need you here, Callan."

"Not yet."

"Why?"

"Because I haven't given up on finding Daniel." Callan stared out at the neon glow in front of him, but he really didn't see it. In his mind's eye, he always saw Jenny as the little girl he'd left behind when he'd enlisted. He could still remember the way she'd cried when he walked away from her at the foster home. He hadn't cried till he was on the bus headed for the airport. Then he hadn't cried again. Ever.

"What do you mean?"

"I'm going to find him, Jenny. I promise. This—this is what I do." Callan decided he'd tell her that much. He wouldn't tell her about the other things he did.

"The police are looking for Daniel. So are the FBI."

"I know. I'm better than them, sis. I promise."

She cried for a moment then, no longer able to hang on to the thin veneer of composure.

Callan listened to his sister weep and hardened his heart. Staring out over the city, he knew he wasn't that far away from her. If he chose to, he could be with her in minutes.

Only he couldn't do that yet.

"Callan." Her voice was so raw it came out as a whisper. "I don't want you to get hurt."

"I'm not going to get hurt."

"Promise."

Callan tried to speak and couldn't. That was a promise he knew he might break, and he didn't break promises to Jenny.

"Listen, you're going to be all right. Tell me about the ransom."

"I don't know much about it. Morgan, that's Daniel's father, took the call. He said he needs till eleven o'clock tomorrow to get the money."

Callan cradled the phone on his shoulder and reached down to his watch. It was the most expensive thing he owned outside of weapons. Combat ready, water resistant to 200 meters, the watch showed hours, minutes, seconds and tenths of seconds. The time was nine thirty and the secondhand moved smoothly and quickly.

"Callan?"

"I'm here."

"Morgan is going to pay. He's going to pay the money and everything is going to be all right. They'll give Daniel back to us. Morgan doesn't want you to do anything that will jeopardize Daniel."

As he listened to the raw pain in her voice, feeling it scrape along the nerves inside him that he couldn't quite protect, Callan wanted to assure her that he wouldn't do anything to endanger Daniel. But he couldn't do that, and he couldn't tell her why he was going to continue searching for Daniel. She needed to think that Daniel was coming back home to her alive, not that the kidnappers were going to kill Daniel as soon as they were certain they were getting the money.

Images of dead kidnap victims scrolled through Callan's head and he couldn't step away from them. Several of those people had gone down hard and bloody. In some cases the kidnappers had killed themselves as well once they'd known there was no way out.

That was a political and religious-motivated abduction. He forced himself to remember that. Daniel's kidnapping was motivated by profit. The people who had taken him weren't there to send a message. They just wanted a payday.

And that made them vulnerable.

"How did the media find out about the ransom? I'm sure the police and FBI told Daniel's father to keep quiet about it."

"They did. They told everybody to keep quiet about it, but Toby told Sierra, his sister, and she was so relieved that we'd been contacted that she told a couple of friends and it was all over Twitter."

Callan filed away the name. He didn't know what Twitter was, but he was going to find out.

"I saw the footage of you and that stripper, Callan."

"Exotic performer." Callan didn't know why he bothered to correct Jenny's choice of words, but he didn't like the idea of Eryn being thought of as something so mundane as a stripper.

"Why did you take her?"

"I thought she was involved in Daniel's kidnapping. But she wasn't."

"The police liaison here says they want to talk to her but no one has been able to find her."

She was currently in one of the bags Eryn had packed. Callan knew the police weren't going to find her.

"They're also saying that you could be in a lot of trouble. They want to talk to you."

"Now isn't the time for me to talk to them."

Jenny fell silent for a moment. "You're not going to stop, are you?"

"No." Not answering would be the same as lying.

Her voice was softer when she spoke this time. "Callan, I know you. I love you and I trust you and you're my brother, so I know that what you're doing is because you love me."

Pain constructed Callan's throat and he had to struggle fast and hard to get on top of it. He managed, barely. "Just remember that, Jenny. No matter what happens, just remember that." He glanced back inside the apartment and saw Eryn sitting at the table looking at her computer. He felt guilty because she must have already started to work.

"I'm going to call you again." Jenny's voice was quieter, more together now, and that helped Callan. "Will you answer?"

"If I can. I've got a few things I'm working on."

Jenny covered the phone with her hand for a moment. The sound of a garbled conversation leaked between her fingers. Whoever she was talking to was upset. She lifted her hand from the phone. "There's a detective here named Vogler. He wants to talk to you."

"No."

When Jenny relayed the news, Vogler didn't take it well. The man's words echoed hard and sharp over the connection. "Tell your brother that if he doesn't come in willingly, we're going to pick him up and charge him with interfering with police business."

Callan smiled at that. The cop's threat was the least he'd been treated to in years.

"You heard him?"

"Yeah. Don't worry about him."

"There's an FBI agent I've been talking to. His name is Dana. Special Agent Dana. He said he's found out some of your background."

Callan's heart stilled for just a moment.

"He seems kind of impressed and worried at the same time. He didn't tell me any of it. I told him not to. I told him that you'd told me everything you wanted me to know about what you do, and that was the end of that."

"Thank you."

"He also gave me a phone number. He says he can be more understanding than the police. He said to tell you he was in Special Forces, so he knows some of what you're going through."

Not really. Callan knew that instantly. Guys who'd been through what he'd seen didn't talk about it. Ever. Those experiences were something a soldier worked to bury.

"Do you have a pen and paper?"

"Sure." Callan didn't work with pen and paper. He remembered things. That was what someone in his business learned to do. He listened to the number and filed it away, then repeated it when prompted by Jenny. He glanced back at Eryn. "I've got to be going, Jenny. I just wanted to let you know I'm here, and that I'm doing what I can to get Daniel back."

"I know." Her voice broke again. "Just—just be careful."

"I love you." Callan hung up before she could say anything else. Then he pushed open the sliding door and stepped back into the apartment.

Chapter 10

Eryn looked up at Callan. Excitement gleamed in her blue-green eyes. "Everything okay?"

Callan nodded but didn't comment. "Sorry."

"Your plate's in the microwave if you want to eat."

Despite the fact that he still didn't have an appetite, Callan went to get his plate, then returned to the dining room. "You're working on the list?"

She shook her head. "Something else."

Peering over her shoulder, Callan saw several digital images spread across open window on the screen. Another window showed the video footage they'd gotten from the hotel. Standing that close to her, he felt the heat of her body and smelled her fragrance. She wasn't covered in soap and shampoo and perfume. There were hints of those things, but he smelled her as well. Maybe he didn't have an appetite for a meal, but he felt another appetite building unexpectedly. The reaction surprised him and he tried to force his mind away from that and concentrate on Daniel's situation.

"I know it's going to take your friend a while to process all the video we're going to send him, but can he work through some of the images?" Eryn pointed at the screen. "I've captured some of the frames. We can send them to him individually. I picked ones that gave the best views of the kidnappers."

Gazing along the images, Callan saw that she'd captured

several pictures. All of the kidnappers were masked, so n
identities were revealed, but Callan felt he was a step close
to catching them. Part of the knot in his stomach was unloos
ened.

"That's good."

Eryn smiled and nodded. "I thought so myself. These aren'
as big as the whole video. We can send them now. If your frien
can handle it."

Taking out his phone, Callan punched in the number he ha
for Koenig. Surprisingly, Koenig answered.

"Dude."

"The woman I was telling you about?"

"Detective Hot And Sexy?"

Callan grimaced, knowing Eryn had heard the exchang
because she was so close. She arched an eyebrow. Callan me
her gaze without flinching. "She took some pictures—"

"Captured images." Eryn shook her head.

"—from the video footage. She thought maybe you coul
work on those while you're waiting for the video file."

"Good idea, dude. She can email them to me."

Eryn picked up a pen.

"She's ready." Callan held the phone out to Eryn.

"He's holding the phone out to you, isn't he?" Koeni
sounded amused.

"Yes." Eryn glanced at Callan, who frowned in displeasure
He knew he shouldn't have cared.

"I knew he would. He doesn't know where the speaker func
tion is. He's predictable."

Eryn continued looking at Callan. "I haven't thought so."

"Stick around. Get to know him. In so many ways, Callan i
vanilla. Plain and simple on the outside, but he's complicate
on the inside when he starts trying to figure out how to dea
with other people. But he's money in the bank when it come
do doing something he sets out to do. Whatever he says he'
gonna do, he's gonna do, and nothing's gonna stop him."

"I got that impression." Eryn looked up at Callan.

Koenig chuckled. "Callan has that effect on people. Ready for that email address?"

"Yes." Eryn held the pen poised over a small notebook.

Irritated by the exchange, Callan worked at remaining calm, but he couldn't help noticing the slender lines of Eryn's neck and how it led to her cleavage. He dragged his eyes away and took a deep breath.

"I'll have those images to you in a couple minutes." Eryn began typing on the computer.

"Good deal. You and Callan get moving. By the time you reach an internet café, I should have the images worked, and I'll have an FTP site set up so you can upload the video files."

"All right."

"In the meantime, has he talked to Jenny?"

Smiling in disbelief, Eryn looked up at Callan. "Yes."

"Good. Now take his phone away from him and destroy it. He won't know how to shut down the battery and the GPS signal. The police and FBI were all around his sister. They'll ping his phone and get a lock on it, track it down. He doesn't know that because he's not used to real technology and operating in the United States."

That surprised Callan. Then again, where he'd been the last few years and the things he'd been doing, Koenig was right. The thought that the police might track his cell phone hadn't really registered.

The smile disappeared from Eryn's face. "I should have realized that."

"You're not used to breaking the law. I know because I checked. And this is why Callan called me in. Deuce the phone and get him another one. Yo, Callan?"

"Yeah?"

"This is my bad, dude. I should have remembered to tell you that."

"It's cool."

"Now you kids get off to that internet café. Uncle Koenig's got stuff to do. Girl detective?"

Surprised, Eryn looked back at the phone. "Yes."

"It's good to meet you. Take care of my buddy while he's in your hands."

An uncertain look flashed through Eryn's eyes. "I will."

"Outstanding. I'll talk to the two of you soon."

"When I destroy his phone, won't you need my cell number?"

"I already have it. Stay safe, Callan." The phone clicked.

Looking perplexed, Eryn shook her head. "Quite the friend you have there."

"I know." Callan handed her the phone.

Eryn took it. "Don't you need to copy any numbers from it? Once I destroy this phone, you're not going to be able to retrieve them."

Callan shook his head. "I've memorized every number I need to know."

Without another word, Eryn stripped the phone to pieces. Callan was amazed at how quickly it came apart. She tore the coin-size battery from the unit, then took the debris to the trash in the kitchen.

Callan took the pistol from the dining room table and tucked it into the back of his waistband. He plucked the bomber jacket from the back of one of the chairs. "Are you ready?"

Quickly, Eryn packed the computer into a single-strap backpack, pulled on her jacket, then took a holstered pistol and clipped it to the back of her belt. She covered everything with a thigh-length black jacket.

A frown tugged at the corners of Callan's mouth. "You're taking your gun?"

"Yes. I thought it would be better than throwing rocks at anyone that might choose to shoot at us." Eryn couldn't believe how she was now accepting the fact that they were going to get anywhere close to whomever took Daniel Steadman, but after everything Callan and his friend had done, she was starting to become a believer.

"Do you know how to use it?"

"As well as I know how to use a cell phone and a computer." She cocked an eyebrow at him and didn't back off an inch. "Should I be concerned about you?"

Callan almost smiled. "No. I know guns better than I know cell phones and computers."

"Good. I hoped you'd start pulling your weight around here." Eryn turned and strode toward the door. Callan trailed after her.

On the way down in the elevator, Eryn enjoyed the quiet way Callan stood beside her with his hands crossed. She liked the way she'd surprised him, the way she'd shown him she was competent at her job.

Then, when they reached the apartment building lobby and she realized her car was still at the hotel, she lost some of the glow. She reached into her jacket pocket for her phone. "I'll have to call a cab."

"No."

"My car is still at the hotel."

"I know. But the police are going to figure out that we're together. They may already be tracking your phone."

Eryn hadn't considered that. *All right, you're new to the fugitive game. Cut yourself some slack and get your head into it.*

"If you call a cab on your phone, the police can get in touch with the driver and find out where we went. As of this minute, we need to be off the grid. You need to get rid of your phone, too. If Koenig had known you'd helped me break into the security office, he'd have had you destroy your phone, too."

"I like my phone. It has a lot of important information on it that I need."

"You can't take it with us."

Desperate, Eryn wrapped a fist around her phone. Maybe Callan had a healthy disregard for all things electronic, but she had her life on that phone. She couldn't just destroy it. Pictures address books, everything she needed to stay in touch with her world was on that phone.

But it also allowed people—even unwanted people—to reach out and touch her, too. Callan was right. However, she didn't have to destroy her phone.

In the lobby, she turned to the mailboxes. She opened hers and Renee's, placed the phone inside and locked it. "They can track the phone there, but that's the United States Post office. They'll have to get a writ to open that box, and it'll be hard to get one before morning." She didn't like the idea of her phone getting ripped to shreds on some forensic table at the police department, but it was the best thing she could do to protect it. She caught Callan's gaze behind the aviator lenses. "We've also got to get some dye for your hair. You still look like you."

Callan didn't take any offense. "Car's more important right now. When Koenig gets us a connect to a friend in Vegas—"

"You have a friend in Vegas?"

"Koenig has friends everywhere. That's what he does."

Eryn got a sinking feeling in her stomach. "Friends like you?"

Callan smiled. "No. A lot of these guys are generally guys I try to put away. But they're people you need to work with in order to get things done."

"Terrific. This night just gets better."

He reached out gingerly and touched her shoulder. "You don't have to be part of this. I told you that."

Eryn wanted to say something smart, but there was no challenge in his voice, nothing there that was trying to belittle her or question whether or not she could hang with him. What she heard was genuine concern, and that touched her.

She remembered how he'd been out on the balcony while talking to his sister. His shoulders had rounded and he'd looked nowhere near as invulnerable as he had while running full tilt at a van full of gunmen.

"I'm sorry. I didn't mean that. I was just venting. If we're not going to use credit cards, getting a car is going to be difficult."

"There was a pay phone at the bodega. We can call a cab from there. The world hasn't quite abandoned the old ways."

"The cab ride can be expensive. So can the internet café." Eryn shook her head. "I don't carry much cash. Usually I use a debit card."

With a look of disbelief, as if the idea of people walking around without money was beyond comprehension, Callan shook his head. "I've got cash. Let's go."

Forty-three minutes later, they entered the internet café only a few blocks off the Strip. Posters of armored heroes and scantily clad women with swords and ray guns hung in the windows. They had a minor stumbling block at the desk because the guy wasn't happy about just taking cash. He wanted a credit card and an ID.

Eryn read the guy's name tag. "Look, Jamie, we only need to use the computer for a bit. You'll be able to monitor everything we do. We're just going to upload a video file to a friend." She nodded at the graphic novel open on the counter and smiled. 'If Vegas had Batman, maybe my husband and I would have had a safe visit."

"True. But only if it was the Christian Bale Batman." Jamie smiled, then nodded. He handed Callan an electronic key.

Before Callan could ask what it was, Eryn took the key and smiled at the clerk. "Thanks, Jamie. We appreciate it."

"No prob."

Eryn led the way back to the computer terminal, sat down and made herself at home.

Callan pulled up a chair and sat beside her, then took out one of the disposable phones they'd purchased at a casino kiosk on the way over. Eryn had shown the CyberStealth company credit card she'd been given, her ID and Callan had paid in cash when she'd explained to the clerk that the company had a fixed limit on how much could be charged. That way the purchase showed up in CyberStealth's name, but there was no bank routing number or credit card number involved. It was the closest to off-the-books they could manage.

After Callan entered the card ID, then punched in Koenig's number, he handed her the phone. "Put it on speaker."

As the phone rang, Eryn showed him how to manage the function himself. He didn't appear overly interested, but he was attentive. He sat quietly beside her and she felt the heat from his leg barely touching hers. At rest, he looked almost docile. His fingers were interlaced. But she knew that he was tracking every movement in the building.

"Dude." Koenig sounded almost jovial.

"You're on speaker."

"I could tell from the way it sounded. Is girl detective still with you? Or did you manage to scare her off?"

"I'm hard to scare." Eryn smiled.

"Good for you. I'll keep that in mind. Just remember, there's always a good time to be scared. I've gotten some of these images cleaned up."

"I'm impressed." Eryn had seen the lab at CyberStealth take hours and days to process images.

"This is what I live for. Callan kicks down doors. I pluck secrets out of digital hidey-holes. Tag me at this address and let me show you what I have." Koenig provided a website address.

Eryn tapped the keys quickly and the site came up almost immediately. Plain and unadorned, the screen showed only pictures hung against a black backdrop.

"I don't have any faces yet, but I will. Or a facsimile thereof."

Shaking her head, Eryn looked at the masked kidnappers frozen in flight with Daniel Steadman herded between them. Daniel looked terrified. "They're all masked. You can't get faces from this footage."

"You have your specialties, I have mine. I've got software that, given time, can peel those masks off and give me a good idea of the contours that lie beneath. If I wanted, I could strip them down to the bone and build them up again. But I'll also have eye color from these images, and interesting little bits like scars and tattoos. This is going to be way better than any police sketch artist can do. It just takes more time. I've got access to facial recognition databases around the world. When I get the faces the way I like them, I'll run them through that and see if we get any hits."

"Wow."

"Wow is right. Don't you forget wow. I specialize in wow. You should see me when I really have time to throw a party."

Callan smiled a little at that. Eryn suspected there was a story, or maybe several stories, that went with the claim. He took a sip from the coffee—just black, nothing added—they'd gotten at the shop next door. Eryn had gotten bottled water and tucked it into her jacket pocket.

"Do you guys have that list of party guests?"

"Yes." They'd put it together in the back of the cab. "I'll send it to you now."

"Awesome. I'm building a facial recognition database off the friends I've listed. Grabbing images off Facebook. I'll match what I've got against what you have, see if there are any misses."

The chair squeaked as Callan shifted. "I don't want to put pressure on you—"

"I'm working as fast as I can, dude."

Callan sighed.

Eryn peered at one of the pictures, examining the exposed wrist of the man in the image. His sleeve had risen and bared a few inches of skin above his glove. She leaned in closer for a better look.

"Third image over on the second row. Is that a tattoo?"

Callan leaned in as well.

"You have a very good eye, girl detective. That is, indeed, a tattoo. The image was grainy, but I've got intelligent software that can bridge pixelization, fill in the gaps and holes with intuitive logic. I think I've come up with an enhanced view of that tattoo."

Abruptly, the image blew up and filled the screen. The tattoo took shape, gradually sharpening until it was a hawk with its wings spread and a knife in its beak.

Koenig's voice was light and happy. "Now that, folks, is not your run-of-the-mill tattoo. I did some looking around after I turned that up. Thought there was a chance this guy got his ink done locally, if he's from Vegas. A lot of the tattoo artists put pieces up on their websites. Took me only a few minutes to find this one. There's a tattoo shop not far from where you two are now, in fact. Vegas is a twenty-four-hour town. Could be someone there is still working and can look up the records for you."

"We don't need to do that." Eryn spoke calmly but she was rushing inside. Most of the work she'd done at CS Sec had been quiet and boring. She'd performed mostly as a bodyguard in casinos and done computer work, putting in hours and filing reports.

She hadn't actually been part of an aggressive skiptrace before, and she discovered that she enjoyed being the hunter. Her pulse quickened as she thought of finding Daniel Steadman alive and whole. It could happen. She was starting to believe that.

"You know this tattoo?" Callan focused his cold sniper eyes on her, and for a minute she felt threatened.

"There's a group of security guards that specialize in guarding high rollers that are known to be eccentric."

"What do you mean *eccentric?*"

"Men, and some women, that are likely to get into trouble as they tour the casinos. CEOs and rich kids with a license, and cash, to play for high stakes and generally lose a small fortune. They're the kind of business the casinos thrive on, so they won't turn them away. But they will hire security teams to keep them clean inside the casinos. These are people that get caught up in the sex trade and drugs. A security guard who gets caught up with these people can go down on the same charges."

"The sex trade is legal here."

"Not with kids and not with people that don't want to have sex."

Callan didn't appear shocked, but she knew her information had set him back a little.

Koenig spoke up softly. "You gotta give him a minute, girl detective. Callan's been buried in Third World cesspools for so long he's forgotten things like that still go on here and people cover it up."

Even as she listened to Koenig making excuses for his friend, Eryn knew that wasn't the truth from the look in Callan's eyes. When he'd left his sister, when he'd left the United States, he'd been eighteen years old, just out of high school. Maybe he'd seen the brutality of life around whatever hot spots he'd been working in, but he hadn't seen it at home.

He gave her a short nod. "All right. Who are these guys?"

"They call themselves Invincible Security. They're a small, tight operation. Rumor has it that whales looking to hook up with the not so legal delights of Vegas can get it from these guys."

"Nice system." Koenig sounded impressed. "They control the customer and the marketplace. Probably even take a cut out of the action. It's what I would do. If I were in that line of business. Hmm. Looks like they know electronic privacy as well. It'll take a while to check them out."

A prickle of fear ran along the back of Eryn's neck. "I've heard a lot of stories about these guys. Some people say these guys have buried bodies out in the desert. Clients as well as *mistakes* clients have made."

"A unit like that could also pull off a high-end grab." Callan's voice was flat and unemotional.

That had already occurred to Eryn as well.

"Do you know where we can find these guys?"

"They hang out at a couple of the local bars."

"All right. Let's go see if we can find them." Callan nodded toward the computer. "Your video upload is finished, right?"

Eryn glanced at the screen and saw that the progress meter had reached one hundred percent. "Yes." She removed the thumb drive from the USB port.

"Koenig, how are you doing with the car I asked for?"

"It's been outside waiting for you for the last ten minutes, dude."

"How will I know who I'm dealing with?"

"It's Ilsa."

Callan frowned hard enough that his brow furrowed.

Koenig sighed. "Look, dude, I know the two of you have history, but I wouldn't have called her if I didn't want you to have the very best. You're outgunned and underequipped over there. And you're in unfamiliar territory."

"She tried to kill me in Dubai."

"It was just business, nothing personal. And you kind of stepped into that thing she had going on over there. I told you that before you got inserted."

"What's she doing here in the States?"

"Cooling down. She got smoking hot over in the Middle East after her dustup with you. Nobody knew who you were when it was settled, but they knew who Ilsa was. But don't worry. She isn't carrying any kind of a grudge."

Eryn couldn't believe what she was listening to. "How do you know she isn't carrying a grudge?"

"Because I asked her."

"You *asked* her?"

"Yeah. That's what grown-ups do. She's in the Vegas area dealing hard-to-acquire merch and did us a solid on this one. Callan, she's got the stuff. She'll take your handshake and you're not out a dime. Also, I know the paperwork on the car will stand up because she does good work. Believe me, this is the best I could get for you. There were others out there, but Ilsa's product is bulletproof. Some of it literally."

"Okay, thanks. You've got the phone number?"

"Yeah. I'll be in touch. Keep me posted."

Chapter 11

Callan headed for the door, barely giving Eryn enough time to grab her computer bag and follow him. She shifted the backpack and made certain it wouldn't get in the way if she had to go for her pistol.

As Callan reached the door, he swung a hand up behind his back. Eryn knew immediately that he'd taken hold of the pistol resting there. He swept the street outside with his gaze. No emotion, no hesitation, showed in him.

Eryn slipped her pistol from its holster and kept the weapon hidden in the folds of her jacket. Her heart thumped solidly and her senses seemed sharper.

"Callan." The voice came from the street to their left.

At the sound of his name, Callan took one big step to his left. "Stay here."

At first Eryn was annoyed by the way he told her what to do. After a second, she realized he'd done that to protect her by putting distance between them. She gripped her pistol more tightly, then relaxed her hand.

The voice came from a black Dodge Challenger with heavily tinted windows to Callan's left. The passenger-side window rolled down, reflecting the internet café's light for a moment before it spilled over and disappeared into the blackness of the car's interior.

A smiling redhead sat behind the wheel. Big curls rested

on her bare shoulders and tumbled down her back. She had both her hands in the open, wrists resting on the wheel. "Hello, Callan."

"Ilsa." Callan stayed where he was. His hand never moved from his back and he'd turned slightly sideways to her, profiling so he made a smaller target.

After seeing Callan charge a van filled with guys using automatic weapons, Eryn felt almost unnerved by his show of caution over one woman now.

"Come, come. Don't tell me you fear me." Her voice was a husky smoker's contralto and it held a hint of scathing mockery. She also sounded Russian or at least Eastern European.

Callan's answer was hard and cold. "No, I'm not afraid of you, but I don't trust you much, either."

She laughed and Eryn hated her a little for that because the woman could calmly sit there knowing Callan had a weapon and wouldn't hesitate to use it. He was tense and she was relaxed. Or at least she appeared to be at ease.

"You should let bygones be bygones."

"You tried to kill me in Dubai."

"Silly man. If I had succeeded, I would have regretted it. I would miss you greatly. Besides, I trusted you to survive. If anyone should be upset, it should be me. You shot me. Ruined my bikini line." Ilsa shrugged. "Thankfully, I am not a model, but a woman has to concern herself over her looks, yes?"

"Keep your hands where I can see them and get out of the car."

Slowly, as cars passed in the street behind her, Ilsa clambered out of the car. She wore a too-short metallic-green dress that clung to her figure and knee-high boots made to be adored. Anywhere else she might have stood out as remarkable or amazing, but she fit in with Vegas. And she was still pretty amazing. Crazy beautiful with wide blue eyes and that cinnamon-colored hair. Eryn hadn't thought that the woman would be plain and built like an NFL lineman, but this was unfair.

Ilsa dangled a set of keys from one slim forefinger. "The car is in a fake name. A driver's license and the necessary paperwork are in the glove compartment."

"Your work?"

Ilsa shook her head. "Koenig's. I merely turned his work into physical documentation. If need be, the identity will stand up to close scrutiny." She smiled. "Probably better than you will. Your face has been all over the television, Callan. Such a handsome face."

All right, Eryn admitted to herself, that's enough. She hated Ilsa just a little more for the casual flirtation.

"You were supposed to be delivering more than just the car."

Ilsa gave a casual nod to the trunk. "There. Everything you should need. I added a few things to Koenig's shopping list."

Callan nodded. "Leave the keys on top of the car and walk away."

Ilsa faked a look of surprise. "What? All business, Callan? After all that we have shared?"

Yes, Eryn thought. *All business. Now put those knee-highs into walking mode and go away, red.*

"A shame." Ilsa looked regretful, but it was all posturing, purely sexual heat. "It wasn't always just business between us."

"I don't have a lot of time here, Ilsa." Callan's voice was flat.

"So our mutual friend has told me." Ilsa pursed her lips. "You know, I have a few other things to do before morning, but it's nothing I couldn't put off. In case you need another set of hands on this thing. For you, I would be willing to do this. I will not even charge you."

"No."

Ilsa cocked a disapproving eyebrow. "Maybe you should ask yourself if you are making a mistake. You know I can be very helpful with something like this. I saw the men on the television. They seem very professional."

"We can handle this."

Eryn had to stop herself from smiling at the *we.*

Ilsa shifted her attention full on to Eryn for the first time but Eryn knew she'd been on the other woman's radar from the moment she'd followed Callan out of the internet café. "This woman doesn't seem to be cut from the same cloth as the usual company you keep. When things become hard, she will fail you."

Eryn almost spoke up in her own defense and stopped herself just short of it. The other woman had deliberately taken a shot at her to get a rise out of Callan. If Eryn gave in to that impulse, that would happen. She kept quiet.

"Put the keys on the car and walk away, Ilsa."

With a small shrug, Ilsa deposited the keys on top of the car. Instead of walking away, she came around the car and walked toward Callan. "I will not leave without a proper goodbye, Callan."

Shoot her, Eryn thought. Not believing what was taking place, she watched as the redhead walked up to Callan, cupped his face in both her hands and kissed him soundly.

To his credit, Callan seemed unaffected by the smoldering kiss that seemed to last forever. He held his ground, and he even shifted to put his gun farther beyond the woman's reach.

After what seemed an interminable time, Ilsa backed away and smiled at him again. "You be careful, Callan. I wouldn't want anything to happen to you. I look forward to seeing you again. Unless, of course, we end up on opposite sides again." She turned and walked away, and her hips rolled suggestively under the tight dress.

Angry and feeling a little humiliated, Eryn walked over to him. "Pull your eyes back in your head."

"What?"

Eryn nodded to the woman. "Enjoying the show? Vegas is full of exotic dancers who can throw it better than that." She knew that wasn't true, because the redhead possessed both natural and practiced skills, but since it was Callan's first time to the city, she guessed that he didn't know about the strip bars.

Callan relaxed a little as she got into a car and took off. "That's probably the most dangerous woman you'll ever meet."

"She wasn't good enough to kill you in Dubai."

"I got lucky." Callan paused. "And I'm good at what I do. But mostly that time in Dubai it was luck." He plucked the keys from atop the car.

Eryn reached for the passenger door and he grabbed her hand. "Wait."

"What?" Eryn yanked her hand out of his and hated the way she'd liked the calm strength of his grip.

"You didn't see Ilsa open that door, and you never saw her with the engine running. Give me a minute."

Standing on the sidewalk and feeling foolish as curious passersby and cars drove by, Eryn watched Callan inspect the car. He started underneath, lying on his back and sliding partially under the vehicle. Then he reached inside and popped the hood.

"You really don't trust her?"

"No." Callan took a Mini Maglite from his jacket pocket, flicked it on and played it over the engine. "I thought that was clear from the way I said, *I don't trust her,* and the fact that she tried to kill me."

Needing to feel she was doing something, Eryn walked over to Callan's side and stared at the engine. She didn't recognize anything in the maze of parts and hoses and wiring. Evidently Callan did, though, because he pushed through the hoses and inspected wiring harnesses.

"Not even after Koenig vouched for her?"

"Koenig is a smart guy. About the things he specializes in, he's probably the smartest guy I know. But he's not Ilsa-smart."

"Does he have a history with her? Something more than *business?*" Eryn heard the hint of jealousy in her voice and she didn't like it. She didn't know what it was about Callan that pushed her buttons like that, but those feelings were just as real as the ones she experienced from his nearness and his

touch. If they were together much longer, being around hi
was going to make her crazy.

"You think you've got her figured out?"

"No, I've figured out that being around her isn't good fo
me. I didn't need to know any more. I keep my life as simpl
as I can. I find answers that work for me. Keeps everythin
less complicated."

Eryn felt a little happy about that, but she kept it to hersel

A moment later, Callan let out a long breath and seeme
satisfied. He closed the hood and walked to the rear of the ca
When he opened the trunk, a light came on and revealed blac
hard plastic cases. A brief inspection revealed pistols, a comba
shotgun and a machine pistol.

"You plan on going to war?" Eryn couldn't believe all th
firepower the trunk held, and a fresh wave of fear washe
through her, displacing the anger and the insane bits of jea
ousy.

"Not planning to. Just prepared to."

Spotting a bag next to the cases, Eryn stepped around Calla
and tugged on the bag's lip so the flashlight beam shined insid
The white beam slid across greasy spheres with attached ring
"Are those *hand grenades?*"

"Yeah."

"You *asked* for hand grenades?"

Callan closed the trunk. "No, I didn't ask for hand grenade
Those are Ilsa's idea of party favors."

The world spun around Eryn for just a moment and sh
thought she might need to sit down.

Callan studied her in quiet contemplation, his eyes almos
hidden behind the aviators. When he spoke, his voice was so
and solemn and earnest. "This is your last chance to walk away
Eryn. Whatever happens, it's going to get crazy."

As she looked at him, she realized that he could have easi
left her standing there. She wouldn't have been able to sto
him.

Evidently he guessed what she was thinking. He smiled

little. "I could leave you here, but I won't. Not if that's not what you want."

"Why? Because I know about your car? The weapons? Do you think I'd just run to the police?"

"No. Even if you did, they'd have to find me. I could be lost long enough to do what I need to do." He compressed his lips and looked at her. "I respect you enough not to leave you standing here."

"Why?"

"Because you earned the right to make the call on your involvement." Callan turned and walked up to the passenger-side door. He opened the door and stood waiting.

Eryn waited just for a moment and walked toward the door. "Things might be less crazy if I come with you."

Before she reached the door, he closed it and leaned against it. He shook his head. "I can do this without you. Just give me the name of the bar and I'll be on my way. I don't want you coming just because you think you have to. For whatever reason. I won't have that on my head."

Folding her arms, Eryn stared up at him and sought to control her temper. She *so* did not understand him. One minute he was letting her go, the next he was closing the door. His logic, if there was any, didn't make sense.

"You said I earned the right to choose."

"Not for the wrong reasons."

She met his gaze and held it. Her body was conscious of his proximity and she felt the heat off him, smelled his scent—unadorned by cologne—and wondered what if would be like if he kissed her. His lips parted just slightly, enough to lead her to believe he had at least thought about the possibility. She steeled herself against that. She was *not* going to let that happen. "Either I earned the right, or I didn't. Which is it?"

With obvious reluctance, Callan opened the door. She slid in and he closed the door behind her and walked around the car. Without a word, he dropped into the driver's seat, keyed

the ignition and pulled the transmission into gear. Darting
quick look backward, he pulled out into traffic.

Eryn fastened her seat belt. "I could drive. It would be easi
I know the city."

"No."

"Control issues?"

Callan ignored her. "Where do I find this club?"

Just to be irritating, Eryn rattled off the street address. 1
her surprise, Callan reached forward and punched the addre
into the GPS unit on the dash. His current position lit up ar
a quick street route sketched across the screen.

"You know how to operate a GPS but you know hardly an'
thing about a cell phone."

"GPS units are standard equipment I deal with. Cell phon
aren't." Callan put his foot down harder on the accelerator ar
shot through traffic.

At first Eryn was nervous, but he had a light touch on th
steering wheel and accelerated and braked smoothly. His ski
irritated her on a whole new level. "They have GPS functior
on cell phones, too, but you probably didn't know that."

"I didn't know that. That's something I can use."

"You also don't know why I'm coming with you."

His eyes narrowed behind the aviator lenses and his voi
dropped to a growl. "My first thought was that you just wante
to be a pain in the—"

"I came because I want to help," Eryn said, interruptin
him so he couldn't finish his thought and make her mad. "N
because I thought you need me."

For a moment Callan didn't say anything. Then he smile
a little and nodded.

"Because, honestly, I don't think I could help you if I wante
to. You're way beyond anything I can do."

Callan's grin grew a little larger as he drove them towar
their destination.

When the GPS told him he'd reached his destination, Calla
pulled the Challenger into a valet parking lot across the stree

He slid his pistol under the seat and glanced at Eryn. "They'll have security at the door to keep weapons out, right?"

"Yes." Eryn pulled her own sidearm free and pushed it under her seat. To his surprise, she drew a telescoping baton from her right boot and placed the weapon under the seat as well. "I thought I would have to tell you that."

Callan shook his head. "Yesterday, Toby took Daniel and the rest of us out to dinner as part of the bachelor party package. I noticed the restaurants and bars don't allow concealed weapons unless you're law enforcement. And most of them check." He opened the door and got out.

"There're too many crazies in this town not to be careful."

When the young valet came over in his ill-fitting vest, Callan handed him the necessary payment and added a twenty-dollar tip. "Keep it close."

The valet brushed the hair out of his eyes and nodded.

Callan waited on traffic at the street. Impatience stirred in him like a live thing. The pain in Jenny's voice haunted him. Tense and overly alert, he started just a little when Eryn stepped up beside him and put her arm through his. He looked at her.

She nodded at the club. "It'll be better if we act like a couple while we try to go in. You draw more attention if you're a single guy."

Feeling her fingers curled against his forearm, Callan knew he liked her touch more than he should. He was paying attention to her and not to the job at hand. She was splitting his focus. "You visit many strip clubs?"

"I've been to a few." She didn't back down from him and held his gaze steadily. "Always on the job. I get tasked to provide close-in cover to high rollers who are male. Most guys seem to have a one-track mind when it comes to recreation time. But the worst experience I've ever had—when the whale I was with was tossed out of one of the finer gentlemen's clubs in the city and arrested—was when I was bodyguarding a woman."

That surprised Callan.

"What happened?"

"She got drunk, propositioned some of the dancers and ended up taking the stage for an impromptu strip routine. She was high on something and I couldn't handle her. Her *friends* got into a fight with me, then the club bouncers. We all got tossed and arrested by the police." Eryn frowned. "It was the first time I spent the night in gen pop. That's general population, if you didn't know."

"I knew. I was locked up a few times before I joined the military. Usually for fighting and for being where I shouldn't have been."

"Bad boy?"

Callan shook his head. "I aged out of the foster homes and ended up losing touch with Jenny for a while. I didn't know what to do with myself." He shrugged. "At least here you have a cell. A bed. Heat. Meals. That's a lot better than some of the places I've been locked up. Breaking the law is better than being a political prisoner or a suspected spy." He glanced at her before she could ask anything. "You said that was *the first time* you spent the night in lockup."

She dodged the question by pulling him into motion. They trotted across the street between patchy traffic.

Despite the fact that they were here looking for Daniel's kidnappers, Callan couldn't help but be interested in Eryn's background. She'd surprised him on several levels. What was even more surprising was the effect of the continued exposure to her.

Purple neon letters proclaiming Bare Essentials scrawled across the wall near the doorway. Smaller pink neon letters underneath added A Fine Gentleman's Club. Ladies Welcome.

Two bouncers worked the door. One took cash or plastic while the other used a wand to search for guns and knives. They were polite but they didn't talk much.

As he paid their way in, Callan studied the men's forearms,

looking for the flying hawk with the knife tattoo. Both of the men wore skin art, but neither of them had a hawk tattoo.

Once their hands were stamped, Callan took the lead while Eryn held on to his arm. Near the door, he heard and felt the heavy basso booms of rock music pulsing through the audio system. He opened the door and stepped into the smoke-filled room beyond.

Chapter 12

Bare Essentials had a feature stage and two satellite platforms. The majority of the seating was in front of the main stage while the two satellite platforms were set up so attendees only got glimpses of the other girls.

On the main stage, a young hard-bodied woman worked the pole like an Olympic athlete. The mirrored wall behind her picked up her reflection and color from the colored lamps overhead and mounted in the floor. She looked like a plastic toy and the futuristic ensemble she was currently peeling out of didn't help. Still, Callan hadn't seen women like those in a club in a long time. Around the stage, men and women hooted, hollered and whistled. Dollar bills rained on the stage floor as the dancer bumped and ground through her routine.

The cocktail waitresses were covered a little more than the dancers, but not much. One of them walked by him carrying a tray filled with drinks. He stepped back and let her pass.

Before he recovered, a young woman dressed only in pasties, panties and a bright red kimono approached him. Her features were Asian and she didn't look like she was out of her teens. "Hi, handsome. Would you like a lap dance?"

Eryn spoke up before Callan could reply. "Not right now, thanks."

The dancer took the refusal with a smile that never touched her eyes. "Sure. When you change your mind, just let me know.

I'm on all night. My name is Mulan. Couples are a pleasure for me. I'll show you a good time."

In disbelief, Callan watched the young woman go.

Eryn pulled on his arm to get him moving again. "Come on. You're embarrassing me. You're acting like you've never been in a strip club before."

"I've never been to one in the United States, and I've never been to one overseas when I wasn't working."

Surprise lifted her eyebrows as she guided him to a tiny table in the corner. "Why not?"

"Hanging out in strip clubs didn't put food on the table. Later, strip clubs didn't teach you anything about staying alive in the field." Callan pulled out her chair and let her sit. "I had other things to do."

"Most guys find a way to fit strip clubs into their schedule."

Callan sat across from her and started marking the positions of the club's bouncers. "I count three security guys."

A cocktail waitress came over to stand by Callan. She smiled and placed coasters on the table. "Hi. What would you like?"

Callan ordered a draft and Eryn had the same. The cocktail waitress left the table.

Troubled, Callan studied Eryn for a moment. "That woman offered the two of us a lap dance."

"So? For a lot of these women, crashing a strip club is just a lark. Something to do with their friends. For others it's a sexual thing. Believe it or not, Callan, some women are just as interested in women as men are."

"Sure. I get that. Sex is a function. You don't need opposite genders to make it work."

"Well, don't hesitate to take all the romance out of it."

Embarrassed, Callan shook his head. "Romance is not the same as sex. Point of fact, I think there's more sex out in the world than there is romance."

Eryn smiled. "You're a surprising guy, Callan."

That embarrassed him even more and he didn't know why. His face felt hot and he knew he should be concentrating on figuring out if one of the bouncers had the hawk tattoo on his wrist.

He looked at her, and his next words were out there before he could stop himself. "You said you used to dance."

Eryn drew back then, taking her arms from the table and dropping them into her lap. "Dance, Callan. That was all. You can work in these clubs and just dance."

"Sure." Callan wished he understood what it was about the woman that made him want to know so much about her. "Did you ever—" Thankfully, he stopped himself.

"What? Lap dance with couples?"

Callan shook his head. He seriously did not want to know. Or, rather, he didn't want her to tell him. He regretted whatever impulsive curiosity had made him speak. She was beautiful, and now all of a sudden he was remembering her as she'd looked in that devil costume and the image was driving him to distraction. "Forget I asked. It's none of my business."

She folded her arms. "I wasn't going to answer that anyway. And you're right. It's none of your business."

For a moment, uncomfortable silence stretched out between them. The cocktail waitress returned with the beers. Callan paid her and added a generous tip, but not so much that she'd be inclined to hover around the table. He closed his hand around the cold bottle just to soak up the chill for a moment, but he wasn't going to drink it.

He nodded at the closest bartender. "We need to see what those guys know about Invincible Security."

"If they gave lap dances, checking them out would be a lot easier."

Callan got up from the table. "I'll be back in a minute." He zigzagged through the staggered tables toward the bouncer standing at the end of the bar. Inside the strip club, he felt out of his element.

It was time to flip the script, get the game back to something he knew. His heartbeat slowed a little as he entered his zone.

* * *

Apprehension twisted like a fish on a hook in Eryn's stomach as she watched Callan. She had no idea what he was going to do, and he was too big, too threatening, to move through the club without being noticed. She started to go after him, but she figured that the two of them walking through the room in a hurry would attract serious attention.

Callan chatted the guy up for a moment, then moved on. Since the bouncer wore a T-shirt and his arms were bare from the biceps down, Eryn assumed Callan had easily discovered the man didn't have the hawk tattoo.

Other people noticed Callan walking through the club as well. Women's heads turned, and a few of the men. Vegas was a playground for indulging in all kinds of kinks.

Mulan, the dancer, dropped by the table while a new woman took the stage. She smiled at Eryn. "Are you and your friend ready for that dance now?"

Eryn shook her head. "Not yet. Sorry." As she looked at the younger woman, she remembered what dancing had been like, the long hours that had drained her and the lack of real support from her coworkers and management. It wasn't like that for all dancers. Renee actually seemed to enjoy what she did for the most part, and her pay every month was more than Eryn brought home from CyberStealth.

"A man like that, you better keep your eye on him to make sure some girl don't snatch him up."

"He's looking for a friend." An idea occurred to Eryn. "Maybe you can help me."

Mulan shrugged. "Maybe."

"My friend is looking for the Invincible Security guys. He's trying to set up a job interview." That sounded logical, didn't it? Especially given Callan's physique and intensity.

"He'd fit right in with those guys."

"Do you know them?"

The young woman rolled her eyes theatrically. "Girl, everybody in this club knows Invincible Security. They are crazy,

get into fights sometimes, but they tip good. That's the on[
reason the owner still lets them come in."

"Have they been around tonight?"

"I haven't seen them, but the night's young, you know? Th[
may come rolling in after midnight. Sometimes they do. Th[
work weird hours, too."

"Yeah." Eryn reached into her pants pocket and took out h[
only twenty-dollar bill. She handed it to the young woman.

"Sorry I couldn't help you more, but you might want to t[
to Bobby."

"Bobby?"

"The older bartender. He's pretty tight with the Invincib[
guys. He's got some kind of history with them. Girlfrie[
wife. Something like that."

"Okay, thanks." Excitement flared through Eryn as she s[
veyed the bartender.

The man looked Native American, big and broad chest[
He had long black hair tied back in a ponytail. The flat plar[
of his features made his face look as if it had been carved fr[
stone. He wore a long-sleeved dove-gray shirt tucked into bl[
pants that showed off his trim backside.

Even though he was busy, he must have felt Eryn's dir[
gaze on him. He looked over to her and stared into her e[
without blinking. He had no expression. A gold chain glin[
at the open throat of his shirt. One of the cocktail waitres[
walked up with a drink order and distracted him.

Eryn looked around for Callan and didn't see him. S[
got up from the table and walked over to the bar. She had[
squeeze in between two guys, then she had to wait until he[
knowledged her.

"Something I can get for you?" His voice was a pleas[
baritone. He held a bar towel in one hand and leaned over[
bar to listen more closely.

"I was told this was one of Invincible Security's hangou[

"Who told you that?"

Frustrated, Eryn shook her head.

Bobby gave her a knowing grin that was pure insolence. "It's been real great talking to you, but I got a job to do. Drinks don't get made and bills don't get paid while I'm standing around talking. You want something to drink?"

"I've got a beer at my table."

"Let your server know when you want another one." Bobby strode to the end of the bar where two servers impatiently waited.

Taking a breath, Eryn tried to figure out her next step. She gazed at the mirror and took in her reflection for a moment. She looked tired and her eyes were red. Stacked up against the silicon-enhanced nymphets in the club, she felt definitely out-classed.

No, not out*classed*. Outmatched. That thought only made her feel better for a moment.

Pictures were shoved haphazardly into the frame around the mirror. She had to strain, but she could make out photos of the bartender hanging with guys dressed in the black commando uniforms Invincible Security was known for.

Curiosity and the feeling that she was about to get a break if she was brave enough to reach out and take it, Eryn glanced round the club. Callan was nowhere to be seen. The thought that he might be chatting up one of the dancers selling lap dances agitated Eryn, but she told herself that wouldn't happen. Callan was like a guided missile when he started working, and right now he was looking for his future brother-in-law.

You are thinking about him way too much. Get it together.

Taking a quick gulp of air to muster her courage, and a split second to tell herself that Daniel Steadman's life was in danger and what she was about to do was worth the risk, Eryn darted to the other end of the bar and walked behind it. The bartender remained engaged with flirting with the cocktail servers. Evidently he was a popular guy. When Eryn saw the bartender quietly dip his hand into a pocket and slide a glassine packet

across the bar to one of the girls, the reason for the popularit
was immediately apparent.

Switching her attention to the pictures mounted on th
mirror, Eryn quickly scanned them. The bartender was i
nearly all of them. Most of them were of him and celebritie
that had been through the bar. Others were of the bartende
and some of the dancers. But some of them were of the ba
tender and the Invincible Security crew.

Those had been taken in a shooting range. The bartende
stood with a pistol in his fist and wearing a cocky grin whi
the young hard guys that made up Invincible Security flanke
him.

A dark-haired young woman who could have been the ba
tender's sister or cousin was in a lot of the pictures as well. TI
link could have been through a person, not just the drugs. (
one of those connections strengthened the ties of the other.

The woman showed up in a handful of other pictures, alwa
in the company of the Invincible Security guys. In one of tl
other photos, the dark-haired woman was joined by two mo
women. One had cinnamon-colored hair but Eryn couldn't s
her face as she'd turned to look at the guys behind her.

The third woman in the picture was a pretty woman wi
her fair hair cut in a bob. Dressed in a gown over bikini par
ies and no bra in sight, she was wrapped in the arms of one
the Invincible guys. His arm was draped casually around t
woman's neck and his wrist was turned outward just enou;
to spot the hawk tattoo.

Eryn's pulse quickened as she stared at the man. He was u
known to her, but he was obviously known to the dark-hair
woman that knew the bartender. Six degrees of separatic
Kevin Bacon was probably in the pipeline as well.

Studying the photograph more closely, Eryn determin
that they were at a party at a strip club. Eryn had been to
couple of those with Renee. Looking at the male strippe
overly developed body, she couldn't help noticing the differen

between the way he looked and the way Callan had looked while changing clothes earlier. The stripper's physique was for show, glossed and pampered. Callan's body was a tool, hard and edged from grinding work and difficult circumstances. And she doubted the stripper had a single gunshot wound or knife scar.

Not that those were sexy, but Eryn thought she liked them on Callan. They showed he was seasoned and real, and that he made mistakes and didn't let them stand in his way of getting things done. Eryn respected that. They all made mistakes along the way that cost them and shaped them.

She discovered she'd made another mistake now when the bartender's reflection stepped into view behind her.

"What do you think you're doing?" His face was a snarling mask of rage.

Eryn turned, searching desperately for some excuse for why she was behind the bar. None came to mind.

In the next instant, the bartender wrapped a big hand around her neck with crushing force. He squeezed and shut her wind down to a whistle. She slammed her hand inside his elbow in an effort to break his grip as she'd been taught. His arm barely moved. When she tried to kick him, he turned his hip and caught her foot against his thigh.

The bartender laughed, but there was no humor in the sound. "You made a *big* mistake, little girl, and now you're gonna pay for it."

Vision blackening around the edges, Eryn bent her knees and let her weight drag the man's arm down in an attempt to get free. He maintained his hold and followed her down. He'd gotten too close and gotten hold of her. Those were two mistakes she'd made. Her self-defense classes had been just that: self-defense. She wasn't a kung fu monk capable of fighting ninjas. But she was resourceful. She reached into her pocket for her keys. If she could fist them between her fingers, she would saw the bartender's arm off if she had to.

Even as she got the keys in her hand, still clawing at the man's arm with her free hand so he wouldn't notice what she was doing, Callan arrived. Eryn saw him from the corner of her eye, and she'd never seen a look so stony and cold before in her life.

Chapter 13

Instead of declaring his presence or his intentions, Callan stepped in beside the big man and punched him in the neck. The blow jarred the bartender's head and he staggered sideways. His free hand snapped to his throat while he coughed and spluttered.

Thankfully, the massive hand around Eryn's throat slipped away and she could breathe. She stood on trembling legs as adrenaline flooded her body. For a moment she didn't know if her knees were going to hold her, but she locked her knees and stayed upright, leaning against the counter behind her.

The bartender swung around, yelling hoarsely through his injured throat. Bar patrons surged back like a retreating wave. Some of the women screamed.

Callan didn't give the bartender time to recover. Without hesitation, Callan *broke* the man by slamming his own forehead into his opponent's face. Blood gushed from the suddenly misshapen nose and the bartender had to take two quick steps back to keep from falling. Callan followed more like a predator than a combatant, slamming the palms of his hands against the bartender's ears. Turning sideways, Callan launched a side kick that bent the man double. The bartender's breath exploded out in a bloody froth. Callan's next kick, delivered by the same foot without touching the ground, looking as graceful as a dancer, caught the man in the face hard enough to lift him from his feet.

The bartender hit the floor hard on his back.

By that time, the three bouncers arrived.

Coolly, Callan turned to them with his hands spread at his sides. His voice was even when he spoke. "This doesn't have to be hard."

One of the men pointed at the downed bartender. "What you did to Bobby was harsh."

"He shouldn't have put his hands on her."

The three bouncers held back for just a moment, tense as bowstrings, and Eryn knew they weren't going to back down. They couldn't. This was their home turf and they had to look good in front of the locals.

One of the men vaulted over the bar with obvious martial arts experience. Eryn tensed, certain she and Callan were about to get beaten within an inch of their lives. And arrested. Worst of all, they wouldn't be there to look for Daniel Steadman.

Before the leaping man landed, though, Callan stepped forward and caught him with a sweeping forearm blow that caught him in the face. The impact didn't stop the man, but it altered his course, flipping him backward enough that he landed on his head on the floor with a heavy thud. As the bouncer struggled to get to his feet, Callan kicked him in the temple and he stretched out limp on the floor.

The second bouncer came around the bar with an extending baton in his fist. Smoothly, as if the man was in slow motion, Callan reached out and grabbed hold of the baton, then stepped forward at the same time to slam his forearm into the man's head and turn him aside. Still holding on to the baton, Callan twisted the man's arm and made him flip to land on his back on the floor. While he was there dazed, Callan put a foot against his throat and turned to face the final bouncer with the baton in his fist.

"Your choice. You can back off standing up or I'm going to put you down." Callan spoke easily, and he wasn't even breathing hard. "But this time I break something that will take a while to heal."

The bouncer stopped himself short and raised his hands in surrender. He backed away hurriedly and slipped a cell phone from his belt.

Eryn had no illusions about whom that phone call was going to.

Turning to face her, but not completely facing away from the bouncer, Callan looked worried for the first time. "You okay?"

Eryn tried to speak, but her voice was a rasp that didn't carry over the sound of the heavy metal music. Instead, she nodded.

"We need to go." His mouth was set in a grim line.

Clearing her throat, Eryn pointed at the bartender, who lay docilely on the floor with one hand pinching his nose. Blood streamed across his lower face and bubbled from his nostrils. "He knows the guys at Invincible Security."

Callan strode over to the man and fisted his shirt. He lifted the bartender from the floor. "Where can we find Invincible Security?"

The bartender shuddered and tried to draw back. The lack of coordination left him scratching at the floor with his heels and not getting anywhere. "I don't know."

Callan shook the man.

Eryn watched and felt certain she was going to hear sirens at any minute. The bouncer was calling 911, and she would have bet that everyone else in the club was making the same call. With that many people calling at one time, response was going to be rapid.

Slapping the man on the cheek hard enough to sting, Callan gazed at his captive without speaking.

Weakly, the bartender shook his head. "I don't know where they are. They're either at their office, on some job, or they're bar hopping. This place is just a stopping point for them."

"Where's their office?"

"I don't know. Check the Yellow Pages."

The Yellow Pages didn't list an address, only a phone number and a website.

Eryn plucked three of the pictures from the mirror. She moved over closer to Callan and the bartender. She still wasn't walking smoothly and her breathing was still strained. Swaying, she held out the pictures. "Who's the dark-haired girl?"

The bartender struggled to make his eyes focus. "My cousin, Gina. She was the old lady of one of those guys. She started bringing those guys in."

"Where can we find her?"

"I don't know. She moves around a lot. I haven't seen her in here in a month or more. She broke up with the guy she was dating. Or he dumped her. Don't know. Don't care."

"Give me an address."

The man shook his head, then winced in regret. "We're not that close."

"But you put her pictures up on the mirror?"

"I didn't do that. One of the other bartenders did. She's the one who took the pictures. She has a thing for the Invincible crew."

"Where can I find the bartender?"

"She quit three weeks ago. Didn't leave a forwarding." The man grimaced and glared at Callan. "You busted me up for nothing, man. I don't know anything about those security guys."

Callan looked at the bartender dispassionately. "I busted you up for touching my partner. That's not allowed."

For a split second, Eryn glowed at the referral to her as *partner*. Then she realized that was as about a sexless term as she could imagine the way Callan said it. Immediately after that, she wondered why that bothered her and got irritated with herself because she had been bothered and because she didn't have an answer.

The man was trouble. And he had definite bad taste in women.

Gazing at the shocked faces on the other side of the bar,

Eryn plucked the bartender's phone from his belt. Then she reached for Callan's arm and pulled on it. "We need to go. The police are going to be here soon."

He continued to stand there and she saw the emotion and helplessness knotting him up. She knew he wasn't in the bar anymore. He was trying to explain himself to Jenny.

"Come on, Callan." Eryn pulled at him again. "We'll find them. They're not here. We've got other places to check." She knew that wasn't true, though. The news would spread, and even if the bartender didn't have his cousin's address, he probably knew her phone number. Or he knew the friend of a friend. Either way, word would get around that someone was searching for Invincible Security and they would know it.

She didn't know if that would place Daniel Steadman in any more danger than he already was.

"Callan. The police will be here soon. If we're here when they arrive, that'll be the end of it. Game over."

He blew out a breath, then looked up at her and nodded. "All right."

As they headed for the door, Eryn struggled with the dizziness that continued to swim inside her head. She stumbled just for a second, then Callan's arm was around her waist, pulling her close and giving her strength.

Inside the Challenger, Callan drove purposefully and tried to keep himself calm. Saying that things hadn't gone well at the club was a massive understatement. The episode had been an epic failure.

He also felt guilty about his reaction. He'd gone into the club with the intention of keeping everything cool, giving himself good odds to get Daniel back. It hadn't worked out. Things in his business sometimes didn't. A soldier accepted that and moved on.

Except this mission involved Jenny's happiness and her future. Callan couldn't accept losing that. He wouldn't.

"We have options." Eryn spoke softly from the passenger seat.

Callan worked his fists on the steering wheel. He didn't have a definite place to go, but he drove like he had no time to get there. He bobbed and weaved through traffic like a boxer ducking punches. In the passenger seat, Eryn strained against the seat belt and watched traffic with dread anticipation.

"Are you listening?"

He didn't want to answer, but he did. "Yes."

"Do you think Invincible Security is behind Daniel's kidnapping?"

"Maybe."

"I know we don't have any definite proof, but the tattoo link is enough for the police to work with."

Callan glanced at her. "Do you think the police are going to have any better luck finding them than we are?"

"They've got more manpower."

"Sometimes that only confuses the situation. There's a reason special ops groups tend to work in small units. They can move fast and work better under concealment."

"That confrontation at the club wasn't concealed."

Callan looked at her.

An expression of guilt flitted across her face but she quickly hid it. "Of course, I wouldn't have liked it if that ape had beaten me half to death, either."

"That wasn't an option."

"I'm glad." She pulled down the visor and checked her reflection in the mirror.

Even in the neon glare streaming through the window, Callan could see the dark purple bruising surfacing under her soft, smooth skin.

"Well, that's going to leave a mark." Eryn folded the visor back up. "We can go to the police and tell them about Invincible Security. The picture is pretty convincing."

Callan forced himself to relax. He took his foot off the accelerator and allowed the Challenger to slow. "These guys will

ave someone watching the police. If we let the police know
bout the Invincible Security guys, they could kill Daniel and
ut their losses." He shook his head. "The odds are better if
e keep what we know to ourselves."

"So they can kill us?"

"If they try to kill us, they'll have to come after us. I can
ve with that."

"You're a scary guy, Callan."

"Natural talent."

"I thought you were going to kill that bartender."

"If I'd wanted him dead, I'd have killed him before he even
new I was there."

Her expression in her reflection in the windshield let him
now she hadn't wanted to hear that. She wrapped her arms
round herself, wincing a little as she turned her head.

"So what are we going to do?"

"We keep looking."

"If Invincible hasn't gone into hiding already, they will after
ey hear what happened at the club."

Callan knew that was true, but he didn't have another plan.
is cell rang. He checked the number and saw that Koenig was
n the line. "Yeah."

"Dude, Jenny's blowing up your phone."

Callan frowned at that. "How is Jenny calling my phone?
e destroyed it."

"Koenig cloned the number." Eryn turned her attention to
e phone in her lap.

"I cloned your number. Maybe you can't take calls at that
umber anymore, but I can. I thought I'd keep it open in case
e called."

"I don't have anything to say to her right now." Callan's
omach cramped at telling Jenny how badly he might have
rewed things up.

"She needs to talk to you, dude. She sounds pretty desper-
e."

"Talk to her, Callan." Eryn flipped through the cell phor
she'd taken from the bartender.

Callan didn't like the fact that they were in agreement.
wasn't *their* sister calling. It wasn't *their* mistake that had jeo
ardized Daniel. Then he realized that Jenny might be callir
for another reason. His throat tightened. "You've been mon
toring the news?"

"Like a hawk, dude. Ear to the earth."

"Anything about Daniel being found?" Callan couldn't bri
himself to add *dead*.

"No. And I've penetrated the LVPD's communications sy
tems and am listening in. If anything bad had happened to yo
future brother-in-law, someone would have said something. Yo
should talk to her. She's there in the midst of strangers goir
crazy. The two men in her life that she trusts aren't there f
her."

"If I call her, the police can track this phone."

"Dude, that's why you have me. I can connect her phone
your phone and no one listening in will be able to tell whe
the call is coming from."

Callan took a breath. "All right. Put me through to her."

"Here you go."

A series of clicks, sounding far away and scratchy, cycl
through Callan's hearing. A moment later, he heard Jenny
voice, breathless and filled with anxiety. "Hello?"

Callan steeled himself and focused on being calm. "Jenny

"I've been calling and calling."

"I had to go off the grid. I'm fine." Callan stopped at a r
light and watched as a line of revelers stretched drunken
across the street.

"The police still want to talk to you."

"I'm still not ready to do that."

Beside him, Eryn flipped through the cell phone's contro
Screens flashed across the viewing area

"Hold on, Callan. Someone's calling."

Methodically, Callan took his foot off the brake when t

ght turned green. He eased into the traffic and kept moving.
e didn't have a destination, but it felt better to be in motion.

A moment later, Jenny was back on the phone. "What have
u *done?*" She sounded near to tears now.

"What's wrong?" Callan struggled to make his voice come
t calm.

"Somebody just *called* me! They told me to tell you to stay
vay or they're going to hurt Daniel!"

"Jenny, stay with me." Callan forced himself to be calm.

"I'm right here, Callan! You're the one that's somewhere
's not supposed to be! What did you do?"

"I followed a lead that turned up. I think I know who has
aniel."

"Who?"

Callan ignored the question. "Did you recognize the caller's
ice?"

"Who called me, Callan? Who has Daniel?"

Staring into the red taillights of the car in front of him with-
t really seeing, Callan maintained his control with effort.
is wasn't like any mission he'd ever been on, but it reminded
m of a lot of them that he'd been assigned to. Not all of them
d ended well, and those were the circumstances flashing
rough his mind now. He felt Eryn staring at him, but he
uldn't acknowledge her gaze.

"I can't tell you that."

"You mean you won't! Callan, this is *Daniel!*"

Voices suddenly erupted in the background. At least two
en called Jenny's name.

"Stay with me, sis." Callan spoke as calmly as he could,
t he felt the strain in his voice. This suddenly felt as bad as
en he'd gone to tell Jenny that he'd joined the army and was
ing away. She'd cried and screamed during that conversa-
n, then she'd beat his chest with her small fists for only a
ment before grabbing onto him and clinging tightly. In the
d, Callan had had to peel her off him and leave her behind.

The foster parents she'd been living with at the time had do
nothing to help.

"Tell me."

"I need you to focus, Jenny. You didn't recognize the ma
voice, but that's okay. Did you hear anything in the bac
ground? Passing cars? Voices? Did the voice echo like t
speaker was standing in a large room?"

"No, Callan! What I heard was a man telling me that unl
you backed off, they were going to kill Daniel." Jenny spo
more slowly now, but it was only because she was having tr
ble talking.

"Listen to me." Callan focused on his words, wanting to
them right. He wanted desperately for Jenny to believe hi
"They're not going to do anything to Daniel. Do you hear m
They're not going to hurt him." He hoped that was true. "Th
people are looking for a payday. They know they won't ge
if Daniel gets hurt."

At the other end of the connection, Jenny cried softly.

Unable to listen anymore and knowing that all he cou
do was prolong the pain for both of them if he continued
conversation, Callan closed the phone. He glided to a stop
the next stop light, then leaned forward and rested his fo
head against the steering wheel. With the jet lag, the anxi
of being part of Jenny's wedding, of seeing his sister star
new life that would probably take her even further from hi
he felt almost overwhelmed.

But it was a feeling, chemicals, that slammed into him
wasn't reality. Reality was in what he knew he could do–
he could just catch a break.

"Are you all right?" Eryn sounded hesitant.

"Yeah." Callan forced himself to sit up. The light turn
green and he got moving again. Only this time he felt gu
and fear dogging his footsteps in a way that he'd never bef
experienced. *Bad things* were close now. He'd had that sa
feeling when his parents hadn't gotten home when they w
supposed to. That same feeling had plagued him when

ster care case handlers met to decide to split him and Jenny
art because she still had a chance at getting an adoptive
mily.

That feeling was there now, and it was raking discordant
agernails across the inside of his skull. His jaw was clenched
tightly that his teeth hurt.

"Someone got hold of Jenny?"

"Yeah." And that just gave him another reason to make
em pay.

Chapter 14

Gazing at Callan, Eryn felt so bad for him that she alm
reached out to him. She stopped herself just short of doing t
As she watched him, she ached for him. What she saw r
was so much different than the man who had just taken
three men like he'd been out for a Sunday walk. She sen
the fear and confusion within him, and she was amazed at
control he had.

"They told Jenny they were going to hurt Daniel?"

"Yeah."

"It didn't take long for the bartender to get in touch v
people he claimed he had no number for."

"Maybe it wasn't him. If the Invincible people meet ther
a regular basis, other people—waitstaff and dancers—k
them, too. Either way, those men are going to be more on t
guard than before."

"They're still looking for the ransom money. What you
Jenny is true."

"I know but that's cold comfort. If those people beco
convinced that they're not going to get the ransom, they'll
Daniel."

"They know we're on to them now."

"I know. They will make mistakes. But they could be
wrong mistakes."

"You can't think like that and you know it."

He looked at her, smiled and shook his head. "Become a believer, have you?"

"As a matter of fact, yes, I have. *We're* good at this, Callan." Eryn pursed her lips. "I think I have another couple of angles we can play."

"I'm listening."

She held up the captured telephone. "The bartender didn't leave a phone log on his cell. No recent calls, no address book. While we were there, I also noticed that he was at least one of the drug suppliers to the staff and the clientele."

"Okay." Callan looked puzzled. "Doesn't sound like much help there."

"That's because you don't know if your buddy Koenig can break into the phone company and pull this phone's records."

A faint smile touched Callan's lips. He lifted his phone and tapped the keys. "Hey. Maybe we got something." He steered through the traffic and Eryn watched with growing concern as the speedometer crept higher and higher. "Eryn has a phone and wants to know if you can get the call records for it." He folded his phone and looked at her. "He wants you to call him."

Eryn punched in the digits as Callan called them out.

Koenig answered before the first ring completed. "What have you got?"

"I picked up a phone from a guy we know is connected with the people we're looking for. He evidently kept his call log wiped and his address book is blank."

"Hmm. Dumping the files now." Koenig's voice shifted and became more solemn. "How's the big guy doing?"

Eryn resisted the impulse to glance at Callan. She studied his reflection in the windshield, watching as the light angles shifted and made it slide from top to bottom to disappear then begin again. "Holding in there."

"Yeah. I listened in on the conversation he had with his sister. It was rough."

"I know."

"I'm gonna run interference for a while. Jenny's still blowing up his old phone number. I'm letting the answering service pick up and monitoring it. If something important goes on, I'll let Callan know."

"Sounds good."

Koenig cleared his throat. Despite his enthusiasm, he sounded tired. "You take care of him, girl detective, and you watch your butt."

"I will. I am."

"On another note, do you know how the kidnappers got into the bachelor party?"

"No. I was in a cake at the time they got in."

"A cake?" Koenig chuckled. "I have *got* to hear this story from the beginning at some time. Does Callan know how the snatch crew got in?"

Eryn asked Callan. He thought for a moment, then shook his head. "He doesn't know, either. Why?"

"Those doors were locked. They're hotel doors. Automatically lock whenever they're closed."

Thinking about that, Eryn realized that was true. "We missed that." She explained to Callan.

He didn't look happy, either. "We did miss that." He swore, then looked embarrassed about his reaction.

Koenig went on. "No biggie. Missed it myself till just a few minutes ago. Either those guys got incredibly lucky, and should have been playing the tables in one of the casinos—"

"Or they had someone on the inside let them in." Eryn couldn't believe she hadn't thought of that.

"Bingo, girl detective."

So Callan had been right all along when he'd thought someone was working on the inside. Eryn considered the possibilities and realized she just didn't know everyone involved well enough to hazard a guess. There had been a lot of people inside the room.

Keyboard tapping sounded at Koenig's end of the connection. "I'll be in touch when I have something to report."

Eryn shifted in the seat and tried to get more comfortable,

but it was impossible. She was too tense and her bruised neck ached. Even brushing her throat with her fingertips, as she did far too often, was painful. "Okay. In the meantime, I'm going to be chasing down another angle. I may be getting back in touch with you."

"Always here. Except for when I'm not." The connection clicked dead.

"What other lead?" Callan narrowed his gaze.

Fanning the three photographs she'd confiscated from Bare Essentials, Eryn pointed to the woman in the arms of one of the Invincible Security guys. "See the woman in the bob?"

Callan pulled out of traffic and swung into a convenience store. After he parked out front, he leaned over and studied the picture. "What am I looking at?"

"See how she's dressed?"

Callan shrugged.

"Those aren't street clothes. She's hardly dressed at all."

"What does that have to do with anything?"

"My roommate dances. Clubs are generally for guys, but occasionally they have ladies' night and feature Chippendales. Guys like that. Those events are usually scheduled in the evening. Dancers work up till the time the guys are brought out, but they don't always leave when the regular crowd gets chased."

Understanding glowed in Callan's gray eyes. "She's a dancer there."

Eryn nodded. "I believe so. Or she was. She must have come off shift when this picture was taken. The guy dancers went on. Since she was an employee, management didn't chase her out of the club."

"What about the other two women?"

"Neither one of them look like a dancer. Could be, but I'm not seeing that in these pictures."

"Does the profile of the redhead look familiar to you?"

"She's gorgeous. There are a lot of gorgeous people in Vegas."

Callan shook his head. "Get back to the lead. How does the fact that the woman is a dancer help?"

"It might not, but the dancers tend to know each other if they've been out here any time at all. They shift clubs, network, figure out where the best tip spots are, the best shifts, where management keeps their hands to themselves, and—if they're like my friend Renee—where they can work in a relatively drug-free environment. It's a long shot, but maybe Renee knows this woman. I'm going to send her a copy of this picture, see if she can get it out there to her friends."

Callan nodded in appreciation. "Smart."

"Girl detective, remember?"

"Yeah. I'll be back. Need anything?"

"Coffee?"

"Sure." Callan left the keys in the car and the engine running when he got out.

Eryn watched him go, enjoying the sleek, easy way he moved and remembering how he'd manhandled the men at Bare Essentials. *You're enjoying the way he walks way too much, girl.* She turned her attention to the pictures and used her phone's camera function to copy the image.

"Hello?" Renee sounded awful and a bit cautious. Her throat was clogged and Eryn could almost hear her sinuses dripping.

"God, you sound bad. It's Eryn, I've borrowed a phone."

"Hey, there. And this happens every time I bring Devin over to Mom's so she can help me take care of him. He immediately gets better and I nearly die."

Eryn smiled at that. The statement was true. Renee blamed the day care where Devin stayed when she worked the occasional day shift. The rest of the time she was home with him, and most evenings Eryn took care of the boy. It was a good arrangement and allowed both of them to mother him, especially since Devin's father didn't want to be in the picture.

"How did the party go?"

"Obviously you haven't been watching television."

"If you call *SpongeBob SquarePants* television, then, yes, I watched some television earlier. Why?"

"I'll have to explain later. Right now I need a favor."

"Right now, girlfriend, you've made me curious." Renee's voice was strained enough for Eryn to know that she was sitting up.

"Sorry. Deal. I don't have time right now."

"Ooh. Mysterious."

"I just emailed you a picture of a woman. I think she's a dancer. I need her identified if I can."

Renee sighed theatrically, but it worked against her because it started another coughing spasm. "Do you know how many dancers there are in this city?"

"Yes, but I have to start somewhere. I thought maybe you could forward the picture to your friends. See if someone knew something."

"Is this for one of your cases?"

Eryn didn't want to explain. "Yes." That was the easiest answer.

"Cool. So I'm like a junior private eye?"

Tired and hurting, the enthusiasm in her friend's voice still made Eryn smile. "Sure."

"We'll need an official swearing-in ceremony at some point. Over a pint of rocky road ice cream. You're treating since I'm doing legwork for you. And trust me, I got the legs for it."

"I know you do. That's why I called you. Can you get on this now?"

"Lots of hassle this hour. The extra effort's gonna cost you extra. I'm thinking I want a nice fudge topping for my rocky road."

Eryn smiled again at that. The exchange seemed like real life, not the maelstrom she was currently caught up in. Real life, ordinary life, felt almost impossible to get back to. If they couldn't find Daniel Steadman and bring him home safe, she knew her life was going to be changed forever.

Then she thought about the violence she'd already witnessed

during the course of the night. She wasn't kidding herself. Her life had already been changed. She looked through the convenience store window, trying to see Callan Storm. There had been other changes, too, because she knew she wasn't going to look at men the same. She had a new yardstick to compare them to.

Renee hacked and coughed. "I'll get back to you as soon as I can."

"Thanks, Renee."

Harsh cracks woke Eryn. She had her hand on her pistol before she was truly awake, and she was surprised to discover she'd gone to sleep in the car.

Callan was the source of the noise. He stood on the concrete sidewalk in front of the convenience store and looked down at the bag of ice he'd just dropped. Kneeling, he took a small plastic trash bag from a carton he'd obviously purchased. He shoveled a little ice into the bag, not coming close to filling it, then tied it off. Then he pulled a tourist T-shirt from the bag beside him and wrapped it around the ice pack, rolling it out till he had a vaguely sausage shape about two feet long. He used a roll of duct tape to divide the tube into quarters.

Satisfied with his creation, he picked it up and carried it to Eryn's side of the car. She opened the door.

"For your neck. To keep the swelling down." Leaning into the car, Callan draped the ice tube around her neck.

At the touch, Eryn shivered. She'd seen how violent he could be, but his tenderness surprised her. His fingers felt hard and hot against her flesh, and that touch raised more goose bumps than the ice pack. She shivered again, but this time it wasn't the cold.

"Sorry." Callan grimaced. "I know it's cold, but I can't take away too much of the chill or it won't help with the swelling." Those slate-gray eyes held concern, and she loved the way he looked at her. His breath ghosted against her cheek.

"It's okay. It actually feels good." Eryn was surprised at

how well the makeshift ice pack took away her pain. She settled the ice pack into a better position. When he pulled away, she wanted to reach out and stop him. She'd felt safe inside his arms and so near to him. She'd never before had that feeling with a man.

"I've got a couple other tees in the bag." Callan placed the bag into the backseat. "That one will eventually get wet as the ice melts. We'll rewrap it as needed."

"Thank you."

He handed her a small vial of analgesics. "These should help."

Gratefully, Eryn took the vial.

Callan retreated to the ice and threw the remnants away in the trash can beside the door. He picked up two large containers of coffee and handed one to Eryn. He kept the other for himself and resumed his place behind the steering wheel.

Eryn sipped the coffee and enjoyed the heat inside her throat almost as much as she did the ice against her bruised throat. "Where to?"

Callan backed the car out of the parking area and swung toward the street. "You said there was more than one club Invincible Security spent time. We go back to hunting their usual haunts and hope Koenig finds something we can use. The clock never stops or slows down, and we're still playing catch-up."

Chapter 15

For the next two hours, Eryn toured clubs with Callan. Thankfully all their visits were quiet and uneventful. Unfortunately, that also meant they weren't any closer to finding Daniel Steadman.

They didn't talk much. Callan stayed focused on the mission, but every now and again Eryn caught him starting at her. At first she thought he was just checking on her, paranoid that she'd go off and get into trouble again. That made her feel bad, and even a little angry at him and herself, but she balanced that with the fact that she'd at least turned up a clue that might lead somewhere.

Please let it lead somewhere.

As the hours marched by, though, she became more convinced that they were looking for a needle in a haystack. Some of the waitstaff and dancers they talked to were forthcoming with information about Invincible Security. Not everyone liked them.

But no one knew where they were.

The continued absence on the security agency's behalf was incriminating. They'd caught a break in identifying the tattoo so quickly, and now it looked like that lead was going to turn out to be correct. But there was no discernible trail.

"You're thinking awfully hard."

Startled, Eryn glanced up and the sudden movement pinched

something in her neck. Callan stood next to her. The last time she'd been aware of him, he'd been several feet away. He touched her elbow and guided her to the door.

Eryn spoke up, but she had to speak loudly to be heard over the grinding biker music. "If Invincible Security is behind Daniel Steadman's kidnapping—"

"I think they are." Callan nodded to the two big bouncers working the door. They nodded back, and it was like predators sizing each other up.

"—then why did they do it?"

"The money. There's a lot of money involved."

"But why the Steadman family?"

"Again, you're looking at a deep pocket."

"Why kidnap someone from out of town?"

Outside, Callan opened the car door, then took a moment and draped the makeshift ice pack around Eryn's neck. He lingered for a moment, and Eryn thought he was going to lean in and kiss her. She felt the heat of his body melting into hers. She took a deep breath and tried to calm her racing pulse when Callan pulled back.

"Convenience. Opportunity."

Eryn started to shake her head and thought better of it. "I think there are too many variables involved in taking someone from outside the city. For a first-time kidnapping attempt, I'd pick a local, someone with a routine that I could get to know. Someone with friends that I could exploit. Before I'd kidnap someone like Daniel Steadman, whose family can fill the streets with hired security, I'd pick a softer target."

"That's good thinking."

"I guess that makes me sound like some nefarious criminal mastermind."

Callan smiled and she liked the way the expression appeared, just for a moment, almost worry-free. "Just proves you can think, Eryn." He looked at her levelly from his squatting position. He looked calm, radiated it even, but she knew that under the circumstances he was anything but calm.

She liked the way her name sounded when he said it, and the praise was nice.

"And you're right about the soft target. But how do you know they didn't already give this a dry run with someone more predictable?" Callan walked around the car and dropped behind the steering wheel. "Those guys work well as a unit. If we're right about it being Invincible Security, part of that ability to work well is due to past operations together."

"Working security. Knowing where the weak areas are."

"Exactly. It would be interesting to see how many of the people Invincible have worked security for have spent time in the hotel. If they've been at that hotel a lot, they had a home court advantage." Callan pulled out into traffic and got underway.

Eryn sighed and glanced at the time on the dashboard. It was 1:38 a.m. The hours were flying by. "What we need is more time."

"Not going to happen." Callan's voice sounded hollow.

Eryn wanted to reassure him. She didn't like hearing the echo of defeat in his words. That wasn't something he was comfortable with. Then she remembered how he'd had to leave his sister behind when he'd turned eighteen. Everything Callan and his sister had been through would have broken most people.

And with this current situation and Callan's inability to back off, maybe they would still break. Or maybe that relationship Callan treasured so much with his sister would break. Especially since Jenny had gotten the call from the kidnappers.

Eryn thought that maybe if Jenny knew everything Callan was doing, all that he was risking, she might feel differently about her brother. Then Eryn realized that wasn't true. Jenny was trapped between her fear for two men, and in her mind Callan was safe.

"What's on your mind now?" Callan glanced at her, then made a smooth lane change that cut off a taxi and left angered honking in his wake.

"I was just thinking that it really sucks to be you right now. Daniel's missing and Jenny's angry at you."

"Jenny's scared. I'm not concerned about that. Everything she's going through is normal."

"It still sucks."

"Could be worse. I could be out here alone."

Eryn didn't know what to do with that, but the thought left her feeling happy.

Looking a little embarrassed, Callan focused on his driving and pointedly didn't look at her. "What I mean is, if something happens to me, someone knows what's going on."

That stung. Eryn knew what Callan meant but putting everything he'd just said in those terms undermined what she'd—briefly—felt. "Koenig knows."

"If this thing hits the fan, Koenig will evaporate. He might tell Jenny that we were trying to save Daniel, and some of what we did, but he won't meet her face-to-face. That's not Koenig's way in circumstances like this." Callan paused. "If something happens, something bad, Jenny needs to be told by a person, not a phone call." He looked at her. "If it comes to it, do you think you can do that?"

The possibility hurt Eryn. She looked into those slate-gray eyes and saw the pain and responsibility and wistfulness in his gaze.

"I know I'm asking a lot."

Eryn nodded and her throat hurt, but the ice and analgesics helped and the pain wasn't so much. "You are."

He turned away from her.

"Callan, nothing's going to happen to you."

He didn't say anything.

She took a breath and hated acknowledging the fact that he could be hurt. "But if something does, I'll talk to Jenny."

"Thank you."

Not wanting to deal with any more emotion and bad scenarios for the moment, Eryn wrapped her arms around herself and sat in silence. They didn't speak again as they headed for the next club.

When her phone rang, the sudden noise shocked Eryn. She plucked the cell from her jacket pocket and pulled it to her ear. Caller ID showed Renee's number.

"I found your dancer, but why didn't you tell me about what happened at the bachelor party?" Renee's creaky voice was stretched to near-breaking. "You were nearly killed!"

"It wasn't that bad." Eryn knew Renee worried about her and felt badly about the situation now. "Renee, I need to know about the dancer."

"Okay, but when you can, I gotta hear this story."

"You'll be the first."

"Her name is Leslie Harris. She dances under the name Felony. You would not believe how many people I had to go through to get this. The information came from a friend of a friend of a friend. Seriously, I would have to do a genealogy tree to show you what I went through."

Excitement coursed through Eryn. "I appreciate everything you've done. Where can I find her?"

"She dances at the Amethyst."

Eryn had heard of the Amethyst. The club was one of the largest in Las Vegas and offered private rooms and shows for high rollers. She leaned toward the car's GPS. "What's the address for the Amethyst?"

"She's not on tonight. I called."

"You didn't leave my name, did you?"

"No. I'm a junior private eye, remember? I left my name. Told her I had a guy looking for a private party. That's easy enough to check out. A lot of the dancers know I set up private affairs that are fun and profitable, not sleazy."

"Good. Do you have a home address?"

"Sorry, Eryn." Renee coughed and sounded more contrite and not as ebullient. "That's where the junior private eye thing works against me. I'm not that good. I'm still looking, but information like that—especially about someone in this biz—has gotta be handled with some definite discretion. I'm still working on it. If I get anything, I'll let you know."

"I'd appreciate it when you do."

"What about you?" Renee sounded a lot more serious. "Are you okay?"

"I am."

"Because Devin would be sad if anything happened to you. So would I."

"Nothing's going to happen." Eryn lied to her best friend and it was surprisingly hard even when trying to keep Renee from worrying. She could only imagine what it had been like for Callan while talking to Jenny.

"Good. Let me know if you need anything else. I'll keep looking for that address for you."

"Thanks, but we may have that covered." Eryn said goodbye and logged off the call. She looked at Callan. "I've got a name but no address."

"We're back to square one." Callan rubbed a big, callused hand over his face.

"Not if Koenig is as good as you say he is." Eryn counted off points on her fingers. "As an exotic dancer, she has to be licensed through the Clark County Sheriff's Office. If Koenig can get into their database—"

"He can get an address." Callan pulled out his cell, punched in the number and put the phone on speaker function.

"Here, dude. What's shaking?"

"We think we have the name of a woman associated with the people we're looking for. She's an exotic dancer."

"Getting into the sheriff's database is shaky. It'll be heavily covered, which is not a problem, don't get me wrong, but the license could be a year old and your girl could have moved."

Eryn's hopes dwindled. She hadn't thought about that. She'd done skiptracing before, but she didn't have a lot of experience in the field.

"You did a good job coming up with this, girl detective."

"Not if the address turns out to be old."

"Ah, but lemme teach you something else. You see, people move and they don't always keep up their addresses on things like driver's licenses, and in this case an exotic dancer license, but they can't get far without utilities. Of course, this girl could be in an all-bills-paid place, but that would be low-rent in Vegas. And…voilà! I have an address. Got a pen?"

The utility address led to a condo unit on Harmon Avenue. High-rise buildings towered over the city, looking like a stand of concrete and brick sequoias. Palm trees lined the street and framed the outer perimeter of the grounds.

Callan found a parking area a few blocks down. He left the car and they walked back to the condo. A Sig Sauer P220 rested in a holster in shoulder leather and he felt more at peace with the weapon there. He'd been incomplete without it. The .45 caliber was his round of choice and Koenig knew that. It was a manstopper.

Eryn walked at his side and got around much better than he'd thought. Dark bruising showed at her throat, but she hadn't been incapacitated by her injuries. At times her voice seemed strained, but she didn't appear to be getting any worse. Fatigue showed in her eyes. She'd replaced her pistol at the small of her back and put the extending baton back in her boot. Anxiety showed on her face and in her movements.

Eryn brushed hair back from her face and he watched the natural movement with interest. She was tough and Callan respected that. He hadn't thought so when he'd first seen her and knew she'd be coming out of a cake a few minutes after that, but he knew it now. But she was a woman. The way she looked, her mannerisms, the way she smelled, all of those things constantly reminded him of that. And it was foolish that he was so aware of it.

"The building has security, electronic and guards." Eryn shoved her hands in her pockets and looked cold. "How do you propose we get in?"

"Wait outside till we see someone headed inside, then join them."

"I thought maybe the process would be a little more high-tech."

"We're not geared for high-tech."

Eryn shook her head. "Seems too easy."

"It is too easy. That's the problem." Callan nodded at the building. "Probably got top-of-the-line electronics, but the problem is that the homes have visitors. Not everyone gets logged in and out. You start asking everyone going in what their purpose there is, you're really close to a police state. People don't like that. Especially in police states. Freedom makes you vulnerable because you are open. You have to recognize a threat, and the threat has to be a threat, before you recognize it. The people inside that building are the greatest danger to themselves."

Callan took up a position not far from the front door. Twenty minutes passed painfully slowly before three people—two men and a woman—got out of a car in the parking lot and approached the doorway. They were busy talking, totally involved in whatever they were doing.

When he touched Eryn's shoulder, she nodded but looked tense. "Don't sweat it. All they can do is ask us to leave."

Eryn reached up and adjusted his hat, pulling the bill lower. "Unless they recognize you. We really should dye your hair." She slipped her arm through his and they walked in behind the trio.

Feeling her arm linked with his, Callan suddenly realized how much he liked having her there. He breathed in her scent and felt her breast occasionally press against his bicep. His blood pressure rose and his air got tight.

They entered the building without a hitch and took the next empty elevator, letting the trio go up alone.

In the elevator, Eryn was acutely aware of Callan's presence. She knew she could have released his arm, but she didn't. She didn't want to. If he'd asked, she would have told him that she'd forgotten, or that she was hanging on to him to keep up the pretense. She was afraid that if she released him, they would go back to being two individuals. At the moment, hanging on to him, she felt they were something more.

You need to get a grip. Crushing in the middle of something like this is not only stupid, it's potentially dangerous as well. For both of you.

Although she tried hard not to, she studied Callan in the reflective surface of the stainless steel covering the doors. Callan was handsome, but he wasn't movie-star handsome. He had that knocked-around look, but he was clean and took care of himself. She liked the way he looked.

The doors dinged and opened on the twentieth-eighth floor. Eryn started forward, but Callan took a small step in front of her and blocked the way. Before she could protest, he was in motion again, striding down the hallway.

He stopped in front of 2814 and reached under his jacket to slip his pistol out of its holster. He held the weapon at his side, the safety off and his forefinger extended along the muzzle. He glanced at her and the lights danced off the aviator lenses. "Ready?"

Her own weapon in her hands, Eryn nodded. Her breath hammered at her bruised throat. She'd never gone into someone else's home under circumstances like this. Her nerves stretched tight, she nodded.

Callan rapped on the door with his free hand, then waited, calmly facing the fish-eye lens.

Chapter 16

A minute passed. Then two. Eryn caught herself holding her breath and forced herself to breathe. Her pulse thundered at her temples and she felt echoes in the bruises around her neck.

Callan rapped again, with the same results. This time, though, he stepped back and raised a foot.

Not believing what she was seeing, Eryn stepped in front of the door. "What are you doing?"

An impatient look on his face, Callan lowered his foot. "We need to look inside."

"If you break the door down, don't you think that's going to get security up here?"

"We'll have a couple minutes before that happens."

"What can you possibly expect to learn in two minutes?"

"All we need is a Rolodex. A handful of mail. You can get a lot of information from that."

"And what if it's not enough?"

Callan thrust his face toward hers and bristled. "I'm not walking away from here. Not without a lead."

Eryn leaned back at him. "Neither am I. Not after we've come this far. But you don't have to break the door down." She holstered her weapon and turned back to the door. Then she reached into her jacket and took out her own lockpick kit.

Callan peered over her shoulder. "You can pick that lock?"

"Hopefully." Eryn took out her lockpicks and knelt in front of the door.

"The locks on your makeup case were simple. Where did you learn to pick locks like these?"

"Before I got the job at CyberStealth, I worked as a recovery agent for an agency that specialized in car repos."

"How does repossessing cars teach you to break into homes?"

"You get assigned a repo, the bank or the car dealership gives you a duplicate key to get the vehicle back." Eryn jiggled the picks, sliding through the mechanism with less skill than she would have liked. Lockpicking was a talent that required constant practice. She was going to feel pretty stupid if she couldn't pick this lock. At that point she felt she might be frustrated enough to kick the door in herself. "Sometimes people get cute with their vehicles and change out the ignition so another key is required."

The tumblers fell into place, maybe not as smoothly as she would have liked, but they went all the same.

"Hotwiring some of the newer cars is almost impossible because of the locking transmissions and the security. You need a key. The best way to get one is to break inside the owner's house and retrieve it."

"Sounds dangerous."

Eryn looked back over her shoulder at him as if he'd lost his mind. "Do you think something like that could possibly be any more dangerous than what we've been doing tonight?"

"Yeah."

Staring at him, Eryn tried to figure out if he was joking, but she couldn't tell.

He nodded at the door. "Are you going to be able to handle that?"

In response, Eryn turned the doorknob and pushed the door inward. Callan put a hand on her shoulder to move her to the side, then he went through with the pistol in both hands before him.

* * *

The condo was a small single-bedroom with one bath, but the location made it expensive. By the time Eryn got to her feet, Callan had already zoomed through the rooms.

"Nobody's home." Callan sheathed the pistol. "There's a desk and laptop in the bedroom."

Eryn followed him back to the bedroom and discovered that Leslie Harris wasn't a neat freak. She kept house more befitting someone named Felony.

The bed was round and lush, with pillows piled high, and it immediately brought to mind some of the thoughts Eryn had been having about Callan. With a bed in the room with them, thoughts of sex were unavoidable.

The mirrored tiles on the ceiling over the bed and the mirrored wall made a bold statement about what Leslie Harris enjoyed in her private life.

"Well, I don't think she's the shy, retiring type." Eryn stared at the reflections of her and Callan in the mirrored wall. They were totally overdressed for the mirrored bedroom. That thought made her smile. Callan, however, looked distinctly uncomfortable. A second later and she realized that he was embarrassed. "At least there's not a trapeze. A trapeze would have made the possibilities even more interesting, don't you think?"

Callan avoided the question. He pointed to the desk over in the corner. "Maybe you can find something on the computer."

The laptop came to life and the glow bathed Eryn. The screen immediately asked for a password. The cursor sat there winking at her.

Callan tapped the wall next to him, adjacent to the mirrored wall. The opposite wall had a sliding door that let out onto a small balcony. Framed posters and playbills covered the wall. All of them featured Leslie Harris in a G-string and pasties, dancing on a stage amid rolling clouds of fog.

Eryn couldn't believe it. "I guess she's really in like with herself."

"Try her stage name. Felony."

Putting her hands to the keyboard, Eryn typed in the name. The password was accepted and the computer chugged to a screen that showed more of Leslie Harris's favorite person. "I'm in." Then she started to cruise through the exotic dancer's life.

Thirty minutes of searching through Leslie Harris's email revealed that trying to find out anything that wasn't pertinent to Leslie Harris's life was a futile pursuit. The woman lived and breathed Felony, her stage persona.

"I don't think we're going to get anything out of this. If it's not about Felony, it's not on here." She leaned back in the chair and tried to stretch the kinks out.

"Evidently she pays her bills online. I didn't find anything in her mail." Callan stood at the balcony looking out. "Everything here is personal. She doesn't share her world much."

"After seeing what she has to offer on the internet, I'm tempted to argue with you. If anything, I think she overshares." Eryn tried to roll her head but her neck filled with painful twinges.

"Can I help?"

Callan's voice sounded really near. She was startled to look back and see him standing behind her. "Help?"

"Your neck. The muscles are tightening up. Maybe I can help loosen them up."

Eryn hesitated, but agreed. Her neck did hurt and she wanted to be in better shape as they progressed in their search. But she found she was also hungry for Callan's touch.

Tentatively at first, Callan put his hands on her neck and began kneading her neck. His efforts were painful at first, almost to the point that she couldn't stand it. Then the heat of his hands took some of the pain away. She relaxed and gave herself over to him, to the strength that worked at her forcefully and tenderly.

When she closed her eyes, the stress over Daniel Steadman's kidnapping almost disappeared. A warm lassitude crept over her and she felt more calm and at peace than she could ever remember.

"Stand up. Let's get your back straight and work a deeper massage."

Quietly, Eryn stood and rested her hands on the back of the chair. Callan continued working his hands along her neck, spreading out to her shoulders now. The heat and pressure was the most wonderful thing she'd ever experienced. She didn't realize she'd leaned back against him until she felt his hard body against her.

When she turned around, she meant to tell him she'd had enough. The massage was definitely having more of an effect than she had counted on and she wanted it stopped. Or rather, she told herself she should stop.

Instead, when she turned around to Callan, she looked up into those slate-gray eyes behind those aviators and saw the hunger in his gaze. She reached up, placed a palm against his face and pulled him down toward her. Their lips met and the warmth she'd been feeling suddenly cascaded and flooded her body and her mind. She couldn't think of anything except his lips on hers.

His kiss was hot and forceful, demanding and overpowering. Her senses swam. For a moment she thought her knees were going to buckle. Then he wrapped an arm around her and cupped a hand behind her head, pulling her even closer. His breathing was ragged, more strained than it had been even after the fight at the club.

Eryn felt the strength in him and knew that he desired her. The sense of power within him was all consuming. Before she knew what she was doing, she slid her hands under his pullover and ran them over his flat stomach and broad chest. She tried to stop. At least, she told herself she tried to stop. But the flat planes of hard muscle and heated body were too much.

He continued kissing her, but his hands were busy, too. He slipped one under her shirt and his fingers caressed her belly and cupped her breast. When his hand closed over her breast, she moaned and bit at his lower lip. He kissed her harder.

Then someone put a key in the condo's front door lock.

Callan peeled away from her like morning mist before the sun. He'd been there, then he was gone. She was only a half step behind him when he headed for the door, though. His pistol was in his hand, and she had hers an instant after him.

At the door, Callan took up a position to one side and waved Eryn back behind the small panel that set off the living room area from the rest of the condo. Eryn was painfully aware that the panel wouldn't stop bullets. She also knew that she could get arrested for breaking and entering. But she didn't want to die. The men they were after didn't hesitate about shooting. She held her pistol, her left hand wrapped tightly over her right so she could create the push/pull necessary to operate the semi-automatic weapon's recoil. That had been drilled into her at the firing range.

Leslie Harris walked through the door still talking to the man behind her. The guy was muscular and dressed in dark clothing.

"Seriously, Sam, I don't see why I have to leave my home. I'm safe here." Leslie reached for the light switch.

"I told you already. Dylan thinks we'll all be better off disappearing for the night. I shouldn't have let you come back here."

"You've still never said what this is about." Leslie flicked the switch on and the bright light filled the condo.

Sam's gaze lit on the panel that separated the living room area from the rest of the condo. Too late, Eryn realized the panel held inset windowpanes and that her shadow was revealed through the translucent glass.

Striding forward quickly, Sam yanked a big pistol from a cross-draw holster on his belt. The pistol swung up in Eryn's direction and the man started firing immediately.

Thunder filled the small room. Bullets ripped through the glass panes and the thin wood. The panel offered no protection.

Panicked, struggling to control her fear, Eryn threw herself forward and dropped to the floor. The impact knocked the wind out of her and caused her neck to flare with pain. Concentrating, she tried to pull her pistol up, already knowing she was going to be too late.

Callan stepped out around the door and thrust his pistol forward. Sam cursed and threw himself to one side, turning quickly to bring his weapon up and around. Coolly, never flinching, Callan shot the man twice as Sam's rounds tore the air around him. One of the bullets ripped through the collar of Callan's jacket, leaving it in tatters.

Blood sprayed across the wall behind Sam and over Leslie Harris as she cowered on her knees with her hands wrapped over her head. She screamed, but the noise barely penetrated the cottony numbness that filled Eryn's ears.

In a couple long strides, Callan reached the man and took the gun from his limp hand. He turned to Eryn. "Are you hit?"

Cautiously, Eryn stood. Splinters and broken glass tumbled from her and dropped to the floor. She checked and couldn't believe she hadn't been hit. "No. I'm fine."

Callan focused on the woman. "Where are they holding Daniel Steadman?"

Tears rolled down the woman's eyes. She opened her mouth but couldn't speak. She sat huddled on the floor with her arms around herself. Then she started rocking, gently thudding her head against the wall.

Callan thrust the captured pistol into his jacket pocket and holstered the other one. He knelt in front of the woman. Without warning, he slapped the woman.

The blow shocked Eryn and she started forward, anger already boiling. Then she realized that Callan hadn't struck the woman with any real force, just enough to get her attention.

He repeated the question in a calm voice.

Leslie Harris shook her head and drew back against the wall. "I don't know anything about that."

"Was he involved in the kidnapping?"

Personally, Eryn had no doubts about that. The guy had pulled his weapon too quickly and started blazing away.

"I don't know." Leslie wiped at her eyes with the back of her hand. Mascara smeared. "I was out clubbing with a girl-friend. She went off with some guy we'd just met and left me there. I was too drunk to drive home. I called Sam and asked him to take me home. He did."

Eryn didn't know if the woman was lying or not. The part about getting drunk rang true.

Evidently Callan didn't believe her. He shoved his face in closer to the woman's. She tried to draw away but there was nowhere to go. "Tell me about the kidnapping."

Leslie gulped air. "Okay. *Okay.*" She swore but Callan didn't back away. "Sam told me they were gonna take down some high roller, but I didn't know who and I didn't know when they were gonna do it. After Sam picked me up at the bar, I asked him about it. He didn't want to tell me anything, but I saw the news about the kidnapping and I kept pushing him when he came to pick me up. He told me he and Dylan had kidnapped Daniel Steadman. That's all I know. I swear!"

For a moment Eryn thought Callan was going to hit the woman again. She almost wouldn't have blamed him, but she also knew she wasn't going to allow it to happen again.

With a brief growl, Callan stood and walked away from the woman. Kneeling again, he went through the dead man's pockets. Eryn knew Sam was dead. Both of Callan's shots had gone into the man's chest less than a hand's breadth apart.

He stood once more and looked at Eryn. "Let's go."

Eryn was surprised she could move, but she could and she did. She'd never before seen someone get shot. And she couldn't believe Callan had shot the man so dispassionately. He'd done it to save her, she knew that. It would have been better to have the man alive to talk to, but he'd killed the man to keep her safe.

That makes you responsible for that man's death. Guilt nipped at Eryn's conscious mind, becoming a definite ripple that wouldn't be denied. If she had been in a safe spot, Sam would never have been killed. She tried to swallow, but her throat was dry.

She trailed after Callan and joined him in the elevator. Only then did he put his pistol away. Remembering that she was holding her own weapon, Eryn holstered it as well.

The doors closed and Callan punched the button for the second floor. "We get off one floor above the lobby and walk down the stairs." He tapped the emergency evacuation map on the cage wall. "We take the stairs down, then get out through the emergency exit here."

Eryn nodded, not trusting her voice.

Callan sorted through the wallet he'd taken from the dead man. He took out a driver's license, gun permit, medical card and insurance verification on a new Camaro. All of them had the same address.

Eryn didn't need a crystal ball to know where they were headed.

Chapter 17

Samuel Anthony Wickham's apartment wasn't as nice as his girlfriend's digs were. The one-bedroom was a typical bachelor's home. No pictures hung on the walls. The television was a large, wide-screen plasma and had a collection of porno DVDs and an Xbox 360 game console. The sink was filled with dirty dishes. Take-out cartons and pizza boxes filled the trash to overflowing.

Looking at the mess, a twinge of sadness shot through Eryn. Sam's life hadn't amounted to much, but it had been his. And now it was gone, ripped away in white-hot blasts. His body was probably still cooling in Leslie Harris's apartment while the police poked around. Eryn shook off the thought. She couldn't dwell on that. Daniel Steadman was still out there and he definitely didn't deserve to die.

Callan moved like a machine. He sorted through Sam's mail, through the man's effects and through the trash. Eryn could scarcely think as she worked hard to mirror Callan's efforts. In her mind, she watched Sam jerk again and again as Callan's bullets hit him while the rolling thunder blasted her hearing. Her hands shook as she rifled through the debris on the table.

"Do you want to talk about it?" Callan's tone was quiet and somber.

"No." She wasn't sure if he was talking about Sam's death or the mutual attraction that had popped up in the bedroom.

She hoped he was talking about the shooting, but she wanted to know what his thoughts were about what had happened in the bedroom, too. Before she talked with him about that, though, she needed to know where her head was. She wasn't like that, not the kind of woman to get so attracted to a man in so short of a time.

And she was attracted. She had no choice but to accept that and deal. Attractions were not good things for her. Or anyone else, in her opinion. Those feelings couldn't be monitored and usually made a mess of someone's life. She'd seen it happen. It had happened to her in the past. She didn't want that to happen to her again, and knew that it already had.

Ever since she'd popped out of that cake, her life hadn't been her own. She took a breath and let it out. That wasn't being fair to Callan, and it wasn't true. He'd offered to cut her loose from everything. She'd stubbornly clung to him.

Now look where she was.

And his life had changed, too. She wondered if he thought she was a complication that he didn't need. Judging from Ilsa, his track record with the opposite sex wasn't a winning one, either.

"Callan." She turned to face him.

He turned around to look at her and said nothing.

"I know you had to shoot that man." Her voice felt tight and sounded strained. "I get that. If things had gone differently, if you hadn't acted so quickly, I'd probably be dead right now."

He hesitated and she was certain that lying about the situation crossed his mind. Then he shrugged and nodded. "Maybe."

"And if you hadn't shot him, I was going to. I didn't want to die, Callan." Tears spilled from her eyes then and she hated them. "I just wasn't fast enough to save myself."

His voice gentled. "Next time you'll be fast enough. You hesitated this time. Next time you'll know when you have to shoot someone and you'll do it without freezing up."

"I don't *want* to have to shoot someone." Her voice rose. "I don't want to be in those kinds of situations."

"No one does. The situation we're in now could be the case that causes you to shoot a person." Callan was silent for a moment. He looked away from her, but he didn't turn away. "Every life you take touches you. Even when you don't know who that person was. You'd think it would be easier than that if you didn't know them, but it's not true." He inhaled. "If I ever get to where I don't feel it when I take a life, I won't be in this business anymore. But I can't allow myself to become debilitated by what I have to do, either. Then I can't act when I need to."

Silence filled the room for a moment.

"Thank you for saving me, Callan."

A small smile tinted with sadness twitched at his lips. He nodded, didn't say any more and went back to his search.

Eryn relaxed a little then. It was good to know that Callan felt the way he did. She also appreciated the fact that he chose not to notice her tears or try to console her. She needed to get around her feelings herself.

She found a small digital camera buried in the debris of porn magazines and motorcycle catalogs on the table. The camera's battery charge was low, but it was operational. She brought up the menu then cycled back through the pictures. "Callan."

"Got something?"

"Yeah. This camera has photographs of the rooms where the bachelor party was held." Eryn had taken a moment to recognize the rooms because they looked barren without the party setups that had been there. But now that she had identified it, the certainty it was the same suite of rooms was absolute.

Callan joined her and she felt the heat of him again. A craving stole over her and goose bumps covered her neck when she felt his breath brush against her skin. She shivered a little and had to resist the temptation to turn into his arms.

Focus.

She did, but it was hard.

Eryn flicked through the menu and brought up the time/date

stamp. "The pictures were taken five days before the bachelor party. When were the reservations made?"

"I don't know." Callan leaned in more closely. "Can we enlarge those pictures?"

"My computer's out in the car. I can pull the SDRAM card from the camera and slot it in my computer, put the pictures on the monitor. They should blow up easily enough. The setting's for high res."

"Let's do that. I don't think we're going to find anything here, and the police might be by this apartment to investigate after they find out I took Sam's personal effects."

In the car ten minutes later and a mile away, Eryn used her notebook computer to bring up the pictures on the SDRAM card. There were thirty-seven in all. She opened up a notepad window on one side of the screen and made notations concerning how many people were in the pictures. She knew Sam's name, so she tagged each of his appearances and who he'd been with.

They took time to cycle back through the other hundred nineteen pictures on the media card. Several of the men were shown again, but the circumstances were different. Those pictures had been shot in casinos and concerts and restaurants. There were even a dozen or so that looked like they'd been taken in an office.

All told, there were seven different guys in the group. Several of the pictures taken in the bachelor party suite didn't have anyone in them. Those focused on the room size and arrangement. Occasionally some of the men had mugged for the camera, grinning like idiots and making obscene gestures.

"They obviously didn't think grabbing Daniel was going to be a problem." That bothered Eryn a lot.

"It wasn't." Anger and disgust rumbled in Callan's voice. He pointed to the screen.

"Felony made the party, too." Several of the photos included Leslie Harris in chic clothing and wearing a come-hither smile.

She'd put on a mock strip show that the photographer, presumably Sam, had captured.

"The redhead's not a dancer. How do you think she fits into this?"

Eryn sorted through the images till she found the redhead. The woman was in two of the shots, always hanging on to a guy with short black hair and a soul patch that was also conspicuously missing from most of the images. "She's not a dancer. That's the feeling I get. She's aware of her body, likes to have other people look at her, but she's not got a professional vibe."

Callan nodded in agreement, then Eryn went on.

"Felony was aware of her body, too. She was throwing it all over the place. The redhead is different. She's not putting on a show. She's exactly what she wants to be, and most of that is aloof. None of these shots show her face. She knew where the camera was at all times and avoided it. See how she keeps herself apart from the others? Except the one guy." Eryn tapped one of the images. "She hangs with Soul Patch because he's the alpha male in the group."

Callan nodded. "He's the guy who ran the crew that broke into the bachelor party. You don't know him?"

"No. I knew *of* these guys, but I'd never met any of them." Eryn studied the man's lean, wolfish face. The man hadn't willingly been in any of the pictures. Sam, or whoever the photographer had been, had caught him off guard.

"This guy takes his work seriously. Makes you wonder."

"What?"

"Why the redhead was there when she doesn't play well with the others, and why Soul Patch let her come when he's all about the business."

Looking at the man's hooded, dark eyes, Eryn agreed. The man had an intensity that leaped through the computer monitor. She knew without actually seeing the man that he'd be dangerous.

Glancing up, Eryn studied the street. "There's a coffee shop up ahead. I need someplace where I can borrow Wi-Fi and get these images to Koenig."

Callan put the car in gear, glanced over his shoulder and pulled back into traffic.

"Hey, dude."

Callan straightened up in the car seat and held the cell phone to his face. He felt tired and knew that his body hadn't fully recovered from all the travel the past few days, in addition to the late hours. Some of the old injuries were taking their toll as well because of the sitting and the lack of the exercise regimen he followed to stay limber. Not only that, but the few minutes of intimacy he'd shared with Eryn in the apartment wouldn't stay out of his thoughts. He kept smelling her and feeling her soft skin beneath his fingertips.

"That was fast. Eryn sent you those pictures just a few minutes ago." Callan gazed through the windows of the coffee shop. Eryn was standing in line in front of the barista.

"I would say I'm getting back to you so fast because I'm that good, but the truth of the matter is that this guy was really easy to find. I loaded the pictures up into the facial recognition software I have and shoved them through databases. I got an almost immediate return. The places I look, that's never good."

Callan shifted uncomfortably at that. "He's got a record?"

"Big-time, dude. He's an IRA hitter who got too hot in Merry Old England and evidently came to Las Vegas to cool off. He's been in Vegas for almost two years under the name Dylan Mott. The Invincible Security Agency is his, lock, stock and barrel. He's got it set up as an LLC, limited liability company, and even provides his employees a retirement package."

"Hiding in plain sight."

"Yeah. Are you thinking what I'm thinking?"

"That Mott may be using Daniel's kidnapping as a means of moving on with his life."

"What I see when I'm looking through his financial data, Mott was pulling in the bucks, but he was spending them, too. Maybe he was tired of living hand to mouth, got hungry for a big score and maybe he was homesick. He could have seen Daniel Steadman as one last big payout in Vegas before he ran back to Ireland. That's how I see it. Or maybe he's going to take an extended vacation somewhere on an island. Either way, dude, this doesn't bode well for your future brother-in-law."

"Mott's planning on killing Daniel." Callan's words hung heavily in the muted noise coming in through the car's windows.

"I didn't want to say it straight out like that, but yeah. That's exactly what I'm thinking. You gotta get Daniel back. If this goes through cop channels, he's going to get burned."

"I know." Callan rubbed his gritty eyes. "Can you put me next to Mott?"

"I don't have anything here. All of Mott's business dealings with Invincible Security are buried in lawyers and post office boxes. I can't get a real twenty on him anywhere."

That was bad news. A sour ball formed in Callan's stomach.

"However, I do have something to report. You know when I asked you how Mott and his crew got into the bachelor party room and you didn't know?"

"Yeah."

"Well, now I know. They had a card."

"They managed to get one from the hotel?"

"I went there first, too, but here's where everything gets wonky. The hotel there has individual keycards. Very fastidious about their security, those people."

"Except for the times they let people get kidnapped."

"Ain't that the truth. And they can't keep out guys like me. Turns out, according to the hotel security, only two key cards were made up. Both of them were made out to Toby Ballard."

"The best man."

"Exactly."

Callan tried that thought on for size and couldn't quite get the idea to fit. "Toby's not someone I'd figure for this."

"Mott could have had a hammer on him, dude. You know this business as well as I do. Ballard may not have had a choice."

"I know."

"All Ballard had to do was give up the card at the right moment." Koenig cleared his throat. "Turns out, Ballard may have had a personal reason to do that. Got something else I stumbled on that might help you wrap your head around Ballard's guilt or innocence."

"What?"

"I prowled through Ballard's Facebook account. Did you know he and Jenny used to date?"

That surprised Callan, then it didn't. He hadn't known much about Daniel, maybe a handful of mentions in conversations with Jenny, before she'd told him she was getting married. Usually they'd talked only superficial stuff, just enough to know that they were both alive and if they needed anything. Callan had never needed anything, and he'd provided enough for Jenny that she'd never had to ask. "No."

"Back in college. Evidently Ballard introduced Jenny to Daniel and the two of them hit it off. I'm thinking maybe Ballard didn't adjust too well to the breakup. And he's having to eat a double whammy. Lost a girlfriend and his best buddy all in one fell swoop. Mott may have leaned on Ballard after he found out about the breakup and used him to get the key. Jealousy is a big motivator, my friend."

"I'm going to find out."

"Figured you would. In the meantime, I'm digging into Dylan Mott as deep as I can, see if I can figure out some leverage for you that will help you run this guy to ground."

"Thanks, Koenig."

"Don't mention it, dude. After all the times you came in to get me out of some hot zone, I owe you this and more."

As Callan put the phone away, Eryn came out of the coffee shop with two cups and a small bag. Callan got out of the car to meet her. He took one of the coffees and the bag, then opened her car door with the other hand.

"Koenig came through, but how we handle the information is going to be dicey."

"Well, they were definitely dating." Eryn scrolled through the Facebook pages on Toby Ballard's account. The guy definitely had some guts—or a lack of sense—because several of the pictures showed Toby holding Jenny's hand or kissing her. That was something, she felt certain, that neither Daniel Steadman nor Jenny were entirely comfortable with.

Callan studied the images on the monitor. Streetlights and neon washed over his face from nearby businesses. Anger tightened his features.

"Is this bothering you? If Toby is part of the kidnapping, your sister couldn't have known it. Especially not back then."

Back then wasn't so far away according to the dates on the pictures. Less than two years had passed between Jenny dating Toby and marrying Daniel. Toby and Daniel had been friends since they'd been in grade school. Facebook had the pictures to prove it. The way people could be seen growing up on Facebook still amazed her.

"That doesn't bother me. People make mistakes."

Like Ilsa? Eryn stopped herself just short of saying that and chose not to—with a certain amount of regret. "Then what's bothering you?"

"In those pictures, Jenny's happy."

"She'll be happy again. Once she's back with Daniel she'll be fine."

Callan took in a deep breath and let it out. His voice was strained as he started to speak. "I don't think I've ever seen her that happy since we were kids. Not in person. Since I left her in those foster homes, we haven't gotten to see each other much. It's always been kind of business between us. I think we talked easier on the phone or through letters than we did face-to-face. We've always been kind of uncomfortable in the same room since I left."

"You wrote letters?" Eryn tried to think of the last guy she'd known that had written an actual letter.

"Yeah. Not much email out where I've been. But I wrote to her. A lot. It just never seemed to be enough, you know?"

Looking at the pain in the Callan's eyes, Eryn's heart hurt for him. She couldn't imagine what it must have been like to leave a kid sister behind to fend for herself, even it had been the best thing he could do under the circumstances.

"I know. But sometimes, Callan, sometimes you don't get a lot of choices about what you can do." Eryn took a deep breath and knew she was going to her Dark Place, a memory that she hated touching on. "When I was fifteen, my best friend, Megan, was being sexually assaulted by her mother's boyfriend. I found out and I persuaded Megan to tell. I told her I'd tell if she didn't." She looked away from Callan, through the windshield, and out at the neon-lit city that promised so much and gave so little. "She told. The police took the man out of the house. But it didn't work out. Almost a month later, the boyfriend came back to the house. And he killed her."

"I'm sorry."

Eryn looked at him. "Sometimes I think if I hadn't made her say anything—"

"He might have killed her anyway. That's how a lot of those predators work." Callan leaned in close to her. "You were fifteen. You did the best you could do in a bad situation. The law failed her. And you."

"I know. That's one of the big reasons I got involved in security. I wanted to help protect people."

"I got involved in the work I do to protect my sister. I understand."

"I know that playing by the rules doesn't mean everything is going to be okay. I get that, and I know why you're out here—why we're out here." She fixed him with her gaze. "But if you're going to tell me that I did everything I could do—if you're expecting me to believe that—then you've got to believe it, too."

He stared at her for a moment, then he leaned in and kissed her. The hunger was still there, still simmering in her and she felt it resonating in him, but the passion was more gentle this time, though no less strong. After a moment—far too short— he pulled back and spoke in a husky voice.

"I will."

"Good." Eryn tried to breathe normally and knew it would be a little while before that happened because her heart still banging around like a wild thing inside her chest. "We need to talk to Toby, right?"

"Yeah. But that's going to be hard. He's with Jenny."

"And the LVPD and the FBI."

Callan nodded in disgust. "Not much chance of slipping in under their radar."

Eryn thought about that. "If we can't go to him, we have to get him to come to us. I think I have an idea."

Chapter 18

Eryn's idea was simple, but required stealth and a tech boost from Koenig. It started out with burgling Toby Ballard's hotel room.

After Koenig infiltrated the hotel and reset the hotel room door's security parameters, Eryn was able to get inside the room with her debit card. They took Toby's netbook, which was sitting on the small desk, and Callan pulled out the drawers, scattered clothing from the suitcases and the closet, and flipped the mattresses. In less than two minutes, he made the room look thoroughly ransacked.

Looking at the damage, Eryn smiled. "I'm impressed. If I were Toby and I received a call from the front desk saying my room had been broken into and my computer had been taken, and I checked my room first, I'd believe it happened."

"Good. Let's go give him a call." Callan led the way back out of the room.

"Mr. Ballard? I'm sorry to bother you, sir, but this is Amelia Hodges with the front desk." Koenig had masked her cell phone to show the hotel's main number on caller ID. Eryn used her most seductive and apologetic voice as she stood in the downstairs lobby.

"What is it, Amelia?"

Toby's interest in her was immediately apparent. That was

one of the reasons she had called instead of Callan. Jenny might have been interested in Toby for a while, but she'd smartened up. Given his Facebook history of conquests, Toby was somewhat superficial when it came to the romance department.

"I'm afraid there's been some trouble, sir."

"Evidently it's a night for it." Toby sounded tired.

"I believe we have your computer here." Eryn glanced at the netbook sitting on the small table in front of Callan. Yep, they had it.

"My computer? No. You've got to be mistaken. My computer is in my room."

"Perhaps you should check on that, Mr. Ballard. According to the man our hotel security staff caught sneaking out the back door, he got it from your room. Perhaps you can come downstairs to check it out?"

"I'm on my way."

"Hey, girl detective, he's coming alone."

At Koenig's declaration in her ear through the Bluetooth earpiece connecting her to the cell phone, Eryn relaxed a little. There was a good chance that Toby would have brought a police officer or FBI agent with him even though those people were there for the Steadman family. If that had happened, she and Callan would have disappeared.

As Toby strode toward the front desk, Eryn moved out of the bar on an interception course. "Mr. Ballard."

Toby yanked his head around to look at her. "Amelia?" A boyish grin followed immediately afterward.

Lothario or psychopath? Eryn still didn't know the score on that particular question. Also, fully dressed now, he didn't recognize her, which was exactly what she'd hoped. "Yes. I thought we could talk in the bar." She waved toward the entrance to the bar.

Toby led the way toward a back table. "Perhaps I could buy you a drink. As a show of appreciation." He tried a big smile, but it was the same one he'd used when he'd first met her last night.

The smile vanished when Callan stood up out of the shadows.

Toby glared at Eryn, then turned his attention back to Callan. He tried a different grin. "Big man, what's going on? The police are looking all over for you. They think you killed some guy."

Callan was quiet and professional. "We need to talk."

"About what?" Toby took one step back from Callan. "I'd love to talk to you, bro. About anything. We're almost family."

"I've been checking into Daniel's abduction."

A troubled expression flitted across Toby's face. "So have the police and FBI. Maybe you guys should compare notes and save everybody some time."

"I found out the team that got into the suite used your key card."

Immediately, Toby held his hands up. "Whoa! Slow down!" The smile was gone now and panic was setting in. "I don't know what you've been smoking, but that is *not* the truth. I didn't have anything to do with that. Daniel is my friend."

Eryn admired the way Callan kept everything professional. He spoke in a quiet, nonthreatening tone and let the facts speak for him.

"Besides that, I've still got my key card." Toby reached into his pocket.

Callan reached out and caught Toby's arm, pinning it close to his body and keeping him from removing it from his pocket. Eryn had already stepped forward to take part but saw that she wasn't needed. Gently, carefully, Callan took the man's hand from his pocket and revealed the plastic rectangle.

"See? Still got it. It wasn't me."

"Then how did those men get a copy of your key card?"

Toby shook his head, but he hesitated in the middle, then shook his head even more vehemently. "I don't know. I don't know if I even believe you about the key card."

"You need to believe me. We know about Dylan Mott and his crew."

"Dylan?" The tension on Toby's face revealed that he knew the name, and that he was afraid Callan's Dylan and his Dylan were the same. "I know a lot of Dylans."

"How many do you know that run their own security business here in Las Vegas?"

From Toby's widened eyes, the question was a direct hit. Desperately, he looked over Callan's shoulder. The young man had to stretch to do it. His eyes lit with hope. "Hey! Hey, Special Agent Lempke! Special Agent Pope! Here's Callan Storm!"

Two men in suits had been passing the doorway looking out into the lobby. Both of them were in their late thirties or early forties. They took one look at Callan and reached under their jackets.

The taller one managed to call out a declaration as he brought out his gun. "FBI! Don't move!"

By that time, Callan had a large pistol with a long barrel in his hand. He fired immediately and the basso thump of the air-compressed shots filled the immediate vicinity.

Feathered darts, two for each man, struck them in the throat or collar. In the next second, the FBI agents staggered and tried to fight the effects of the drug skating through their systems. Then they went down in loose-jointed sprawls and pandemonium erupted inside the bar and the lobby. The tranquilizer gun had come in Koenig's care package.

Callan looked back for Toby, but the man had gone. He glanced at Eryn. "Where did Toby go?"

She shook her head helplessly and swore to herself. "I lost him. I was watching them." She gazed around but didn't see Toby anywhere. He hadn't wasted any time departing the premises, but she didn't know if that testified to fear or guilt.

The excitement inside the bar spilled over into a full-fledged panic that sent several patrols scurrying for the doors or hiding under their tables.

"We've got to go." Callan took Eryn by the arm and hurried

her toward the door. "Security's going to lock the hotel down tight."

Already in motion, Eryn sidestepped a little and made a frantic grab at the netbook computer and case they'd taken from Toby's hotel room. She stayed close to Callan as they headed through the door and back out onto the Strip.

"I need to talk to her now." Callan pulled the car into the parking lot of a twenty-four-hour copy store as he talked to Koenig. Eryn nodded at him to let him know she could get the internet. He kept himself calm, but things weren't breaking in the pursuit the way he needed them to. There was something he was missing and he knew it. He was dancing all around the string that bound everything together. A kidnapping wasn't a confined event. There were generally things that bound it.

"Okay, dude. Your funeral. I'm patching you through. I'm protecting your number from her, though. We don't want the police tracking you."

Callan took a deep breath and watched Eryn work the keyboard. Anxiety clawed through him. There were too many variables in play and he didn't have control over enough of them. All he could do was keep digging to try to close the distance. The dashboard clock showed the time as 4:27 a.m. The time he had to find Daniel was growing thin. Six and a half hours wasn't enough.

"Hello? Callan?" Jenny was almost breathless with emotion. "What are you doing?"

"I can't talk long. I wanted you to know that we're still trying to find Daniel. We think we know who has him."

Listening to his sister weep, Callan hardened his heart and focused on the mission. It was a mission. He couldn't think of his pursuit of Daniel's kidnappers in any other fashion. He had to be focused like it was a job, not something personal. "This will all be over soon, Jenny. We just need to hang in there. But first I need to know, before you got involved with Daniel, you were dating Toby?"

"There's not much to tell. I met him at a club near the college. We dated for a while. Then one night we went out with Daniel and Sierra. Sierra is Toby's sister. Daniel and Sierra were into each other at the time. Daniel and I decided we liked each other more than we did anyone else. After a while, we started dating."

"How did Toby take it?"

"You mean, did he get all psycho?"

"Yeah."

"No." Jenny sounded sure of herself, but Callan knew she could also be wrong in her assessment. "He was hurt, a little. His ego more than his heart. But not much. I've never met the girl that could break Toby's heart. Not even me. He still teases Daniel about dating me first, but that's all it is. A goof. Daniel always teased him about dating his sister. Part of the friendly rivalry they've always had."

"Where's Toby now?"

"Gone. You scared him, Callan, and Daniel's father is angry with him for not stopping you. As if. *Ever.* Daniel's father doesn't know you." Jenny managed a small chuckle over that. "But the police are looking for you. They don't want to just talk to you anymore. They intend to arrest you. They're saying you killed somebody."

"Just focus on getting Daniel back. We're going to make it through this. We've made it through everything else we've had to deal with."

Jenny was crying again. "I don't know, Callan. Before, we always had each other. Then you went away. I'm sorry, but it doesn't feel like you've ever really come back."

That hurt. Callan froze the pain and pushed it away. "Stay strong, Jenny." He clicked the phone off and lay back in the seat. Fatigue chewed at him, fraying his mind.

Wordlessly, Eryn reached over to him and placed her hand on his. Her blue-green eyes met his gaze and he saw the worry in her face. "You okay, soldier?"

"I'm holding my own." But he folded her hand in his and

held on to her, drawing strength he hadn't known he would find there. Usually on a mission behind enemy lines, he felt alone. Even with men he trusted with his life. With Eryn, though, he felt differently, and that made him uncomfortable in a way he'd never before known.

Less than forty minutes later, using the software Koenig had uploaded to her computer, Eryn hacked the security on Toby's netbook and rifled his files while Callan sat the steering wheel drinking coffee.

Since the conversation with Jenny, he'd gotten quiet and she knew he was in a bad place mentally. Emotionally he seemed to have pushed everything away and wasn't dealing with the situation. Her heart went out to him, but she knew he wouldn't tolerate empathy at the moment. She wouldn't have, either.

Since she'd already seen Toby's Facebook pictures, she opened up the image databases on the netbook. As it turned out, Toby had the same potentially unhealthy narcissistic interests as Leslie "Felony" Harris had. Toby's world revolved around all things Toby.

She started with the latest pictures first and went back. She didn't have to go back more than a few days to find a link. When she did, at first she couldn't believe it. She magnified one of the pictures to fill the screen, then turned the computer around to face Callan.

"See anybody you recognize?"

Callan sat up and came to attention almost at once.

The picture had been taken at a strip club. That was evident from the nearly naked dancers that Toby Ballard was mugging with. A few of the shots showed the club's name in neon tubing behind the stage: Black Dice.

In a few of the shots, though, Dylan Mott and his men sat at the table where the photographer had sat. In a few others, Mott and Toby had been talking and drinking. Toby's tie hung askew and he wore a big, drunken smile.

Callan reached for the ignition and his phone. He punched speed dial as he put the transmission into gear. "Koenig?"

The Challenger leaped out onto the Strip like a predator among sheep. Eryn's stomach twisted a little with dread, but she felt hopeful as well. They all needed resolution, but at the same time she didn't want it to come too soon because it meant there would be no more reasons to hang around Callan.

"Okay, dude, I missed this little mecca. Black Dice is a new enterprise for Dylan Mott. The business isn't located in his regular portfolio. If I'd had the time to do a deeper background, I would have found it."

Callan sat in the car at a convenience store across the street from the strip club/casino. The small building was divided into two businesses that sat side by side. Both businesses were named Black Dice. One was a gentlemen's club and the other was a small casino featuring slots and blackjack. The clientele was definitely blue-collar and desperate, not the people that were drawn to the big casinos.

Checking the neighborhood, Callan didn't see any police cars or unmarked surveillance vehicles. He'd developed an almost supernatural radar for those things in foreign countries. In the United States, those vehicles stood out even more strongly to him.

Apparently no one else had made the connect to Dylan Mott and his associates. He let out a tense breath. "We're still ahead of the curve. The police don't have a line on Mott or this place yet. Now we have to find out if Mott is here."

"So what's the plan?"

Callan sat quietly for a moment, not liking what he was about to say. He checked his watch. It was 5:17 a.m. His eyes burned from lack of sleep. "We watch. And we wait. This is all we have to work with."

"Do you think Daniel is inside?" Eryn spoke softly.

"I don't know. We're only going to get one chance at this. If we blow it, Mott is going to stay away from here."

"He may be inside now."

"We have time. A little. For now we'll invest it in learning more. It's still over five hours till the ransom drop. We have time." Callan repeated the statement in an effort to make himself believe that. He leaned forward and started the car. "Get out a pencil and paper. We're going to take down all the license plates of the vehicles in the parking lot. Koenig can run them, see if we can tie any of the vehicles to Mott."

"I don't need a pencil and paper." Eryn held up a digital camera.

Callan nodded and engaged the transmission. They joined the traffic, then flowed into the Black Dice parking area.

Chapter 19

At a few minutes till six, Callan and Eryn were checked into a cheap motel near Black Dice. From where they were on the third floor, they had a clear view of the casino/gentlemen's club on two sides behind the building. Koenig had hacked into the traffic cams on the cross streets and covered the other two sides.

Eryn knew the observation post was far from perfect, but it was as close as they could make it. Callan had brought up a pair of high-powered binoculars and an equal quality camera with a huge telescopic lens. Knowing that both of them needed more than coffee to survive on, Eryn went downstairs and down the block to a small café where she bought two big breakfasts with pancakes, sausages, eggs and fresh fruit. She added a large thermos of coffee.

They moved the room's small desk over by the window so they could continue to watch Black Dice while they ate. Callan ate mechanically, neatly cutting up the food before popping it into his mouth.

Eryn watched him as much as she watched the Black Dice. An extra pair of eyes on the building was overkill at the moment, so she didn't feel she was letting him down. The way he moved the knife and fork, unerringly picking up the food without looking at it, was amazing. And he did it all without speaking.

"I guess you don't talk a lot at your meals."

"Not when I'm working." Callan didn't look at her for a moment, then he glanced back at her. "Sorry. I don't mean to be rude. To answer your question, no, I don't have a lot of company."

"After everything we've been through tonight, you owe me. Big-time."

His face darkened a little at that. "Once we get on the other side of this, just figure up your bill. I'll pay whatever you want."

"I only want one thing, Callan." She placed her hand on top of his. "When this is over, because it'll be over soon and we're both going to survive, I want to take you to dinner. Someplace nice where things don't explode and people don't shoot at you. I think we both deserve that."

He shook his head at once. "No."

She started to draw her hand away, but he captured her fingers in his and held her fast with tender strength.

"I'm going to take *you* to dinner. I'm old-fashioned about a lot of things. No woman, outside of a commanding officer, has ever bought me a meal."

"Well, I still think you can be retrained." She squeezed his hand and the heat that had been building inside her broke, and just like that breakfast was over.

Callan stood and pulled her from the chair till she was pressed against his chest. Her breath caught in her throat as he bent down and kissed her hard, and her body was instantly aflame, as though hours hadn't passed since earlier in Leslie Harris's bedroom. She pressed herself against him, feeling her body heating up even more. Losing control, feeling his body responding against hers, she tried to pull him into her.

Managing some bit of control from some hidden recess, Callan managed to pull away. Eryn felt she'd been ripped apart. His voice was hard and raspy when he spoke. "If you want this to stop, now's the time to say so."

"Don't you dare stop." Eryn grabbed his shirt in both fists and pulled him toward the bed. She fell back and he came down on top of her. His muscular body covered hers from the tips of her toes to her lips. They fumbled with their clothing, pulling it away, getting closer and closer together. His hands roamed her body, delivering pleasure to her in ways she'd never before experienced. It was like her body was waking up more than it had ever been awake. Every nerve ending suddenly seemed alive on a whole new level.

She kissed him, bit at him, too, and he groaned at the rough contact, somehow managing to handle her because she felt out of control. Her body opened to him and she felt the warm liquid heat of herself ready for everything he could give her.

But he stopped and held back.

Eryn growled. "Don't. Stop."

"We don't have anything."

"I thought you were prepared for everything." She barely resisted grinning up at his helplessness.

"Not this."

Eryn laughed at him, putting a hand over her mouth when she saw the look of anguish manifesting on his face as he started to pull away from her. She roped an arm behind his neck and held him in place. "As you were, soldier. Maybe you aren't prepared, but I am. There was a drugstore next to the café." She reached down to the floor, snared her jeans, and took out the small brown paper bag that held the condoms she'd bought.

"You planned this?" He looked as if he didn't know how he was supposed to take that.

"You think I'm seducing you? As I recall, you made the opening move on this soiree, mister." Eryn delicately shook the paper bag. "Now, are you going to follow through?"

He reached for the bag.

She knocked his hand away, reached inside and took out one of the foil packages. It took her a moment to get the package open and her lack of expertise was almost embarrassing. But then she used both her hands to put it on his girth and he struggled to maintain control as his hips automatically bucked, seeking her.

Then he was inside her, penetrating her deeply, filling her up. All her teasing was forgotten as her own self-control exploded. She moved against him, holding on to him tightly as he hammered into her. There was no way this first time was going to be gentle or controlled. Not with the fire that had been simmering between them.

Her first climax swelled up inside her and she nearly blacked out. She didn't even have time to regroup before the next overwhelmed her as well. He plateaued at the same time she hit her third mind-draining pleasure high.

He collapsed onto her, then tried to roll away. She held on to him, making him stay where he was. She felt warm and wonderful, totally relaxed, and somewhere in there her satisfaction robbed her of her consciousness.

Panic thrummed through Eryn when she realized she'd fallen asleep. She sat bolt upright in the bed when she saw bright sunlight streaming through the motel window. Evidently Callan had covered her with the blankets from the other side of the bed because they fell away from her.

Fully clothed, he sat at the window. He turned around to face her and smiled. "Take it easy."

"How long have I been asleep?"

"Not long."

Feeling a little self-conscious, Eryn wrapped a blanket over herself. She brushed at her hair, trying to bring it back into some semblance of order. "Anything happening with Mott?"

"Not yet."

Leaning down beside the bed, Eryn pulled her cell from her pants. It was almost eight. She'd been asleep longer than Callan had said, or their prenap activities had taken longer. Thinking about that, she realized that no matter how long those activities had lasted, they hadn't been enough.

She missed the postcoital cuddling, but under the circumstances, she could forgive Callan for getting back out of bed.

She just didn't know how he'd found the strength. She had been exhausted.

"I'm going to shower. Let me know if something changes. I won't be long."

He nodded.

Eryn slid off the bed, grabbed her clothing and her emergency makeup kit from her jacket and headed for the small bathroom. Thankfully, she didn't have to look over her shoulder to see if he was looking at her as she went. There was a mirror on the wall over the small sink.

He was checking her out as she crossed the room, and from the look on his face, he still wanted her as badly as she wanted him. She smiled to herself.

Callan sat at the window and tried not to think about how out of control his life was. He felt delicately balanced, like he was walking a tightrope. Dealing with Jenny and with Daniel's kidnapping had been hard enough. Now with the *thing* that had happened between Eryn and him, he didn't feel he had a handle on anything. It was like he was in freefall, scrambling during a busted play.

Only the experience wasn't as alarming as he'd thought it would be. The chemistry that had bubbled up with the woman had been surprising and undeniable. He'd had to have her, and he wanted her again. If they'd been someplace where nothing was going on, he wouldn't have let her out of that bed for days.

That thought was entirely too pleasant to think about. And there was no indication that anything like that would happen again. That possibility left him unsettled. He didn't know how they could experience what they'd just experienced and just walk away. He wanted to know—

His cell vibrated on the table at his elbow. He picked it up and flipped it open. "Yeah."

"Dude, it may be time to go hunting. Toby Ballard just showed up at Black Dice. He's parking his rental in the parking lot now."

Picking up the binoculars, Callan trained them on the parking lot. The angle was almost too sharp for him to see clearly, but he saw the SUV sliding into a parking spot. "You're sure it's Toby?"

"I tracked his credit cards. He got a rental there in Vegas. The rental has a LoJack system. I've been following him for the past forty minutes, waiting for him to light somewhere."

"I don't know what a LoJack system is."

Koenig sighed. "Dude, we have got to bring you into this century. A LoJack system is part of a satellite tracking network. Car rental agencies and regular people use them as theft deterrents."

"Understood and appreciated." Watching through the binoculars, Callan watched Toby cross the parking area. One of the men from the photographs in Leslie Harris's computer and in Toby's computer stepped from the club's side door.

"Okay, I'm going in." Shaking off the tension that filled him, Callan took a few deep breaths to reoxygenate his blood. His fatigue dropped away.

Eryn came out of the bathroom. She stopped and looked at him as he slid his pistol into its holster. "Something happened."

"Toby Ballard just showed up at the club. One of the guys we've identified as Mott's crew was waiting for him."

"What are you going to do?"

"Go inside. Find Daniel, if he's there, and get him out."

Eryn shook her head. "You can't just walk in, Callan. They'll be looking for you. They'll see you coming. You won't make it out of there alive, and neither will Daniel."

Callan hesitated, knowing what she said was true. Inside the club they'd have the home-field advantage. The only thing that balanced that was that Callan wasn't a cop.

Her face firmed in resolve. "I can get you in."

Immediately, Callan shook his head. "Too dangerous."

She put her hands on her hips. "More dangerous for me than for you?" She shook her head. "I don't think so."

"I don't want you to get hurt." Callan spoke calmly, but just mentioning the possibility that something might happen to her was difficult. "I didn't bring you along for this."

"You didn't bring me along. I brought myself along. And as I recall, we wouldn't have been here if I hadn't pulled my weight. That's who I am, Callan. I pull my own weight. And I'm going to do it now or you're going to have a fight before you walk out that door."

Looking at her, seeing the determination on her face, Callan knew she meant what she said.

"You didn't give me a choice about becoming part of this at the beginning, so now I'm not giving you a choice about how your part is going to go at the end. If you go straight on at Mott and his crew, innocent people are going to get hurt. Not just Daniel. Those people inside that building are going to become targets, too. Unless we can contain them."

Callan folded his arms and waited. "So what's the plan?"

Chapter 20

If you'd have had more time, you could have come up with a good plan. Or at least a better one. Because this is so not a good plan. Eryn walked to the front of the gentlemen's club and smiled at the thick-necked bouncer standing there. Prison tats showed above the shirt collar.

"I'm Aruba."

"Aruba." The man stretched the name out, smiling slightly. "Lovely name. Lovely lady. Nice to meet you, Aruba."

"I'm here about the job." Eryn unfolded the printout she'd made of the ad she'd found online. Black Dice was looking for dancers, which hadn't been a surprise. Most erotic dance clubs were looking for new blood all the time. Dancers got mad and quit, got arrested, got stoned or drunk and didn't make it in. Turnover was high.

"Shantell ain't here." The bouncer gave Eryn a long look from top to bottom. "Won't be in till ten." He checked his watch. "You still got about an hour and a half to wait." He smiled. "But she'll like what she sees when she gets here. We have similar tastes."

"Good to know. Nothing like a vote of confidence from someone with taste." Eryn forced a smile onto her face. The guy's heavy-handedness was off-putting, but the danger she was stepping into was even more of a buzzkill. She looked hopeful. "Maybe I could wait inside. Save me from taking a cab two ways and killing time somewhere else. I can also talk to some of the other dancers. Find out about the clientele and shifts."

That was a strategy a lot of dancers and restaurant servers used. Getting a job wasn't the goal of those people. Getting a *good* job was. That meant finding out how good the tips were, when the peak business took place.

"Sure. Go on in." The bouncer leaned back and opened the door for her. "My name's Frankie."

"Nice to meet you, Frankie." Eryn turned and walked into the waiting lobby, then to the club room beyond.

"There's a guy just behind the door, too." Eryn had let her hair hang down and it covered the Bluetooth earpiece she wore.

"Armed?" Impatience vibrated in Callan's voice.

"Yes. Hip holster."

Like the first man, the second also had prison tats. He followed her with his gaze, stripping her with every step. Eryn ignored him and worked on describing the club and the people to Callan.

The club only had one stage and it was on the east wall, to the immediate left of the main entrance. Despite the fact that Vegas was a twenty-four-hour town, the morning business was slow. The dancer on the stage moved at a halfhearted pace and the three guys sitting on pervert row seemed more interested in their beer and conversation than the woman.

The bar was opposite the stage. A heavyset bartender leaned against the bar with a towel thrown over one shoulder. His attention was focused on a small television behind the bar that was showing ESPN. One of the men Eryn recognized as a member of the suspected kidnapping team sat at a stool at the bar and watched television as well. He poured himself another drink from a bottle sitting in front of him.

"One of Mott's crew is at the bar. To the right of the entrance." Eryn walked past the bar and headed down a small corridor on the right that advertised bathrooms.

At the end of the hallway was a door with Office written on

it. The bathrooms were on the right, and another door marked Dressing Room—Dancers Only was just past them.

On the left side of the hallway, an emergency door opened onto the alley behind the building. A panic bar locked the exit tight. At the end of the hallway, men's voices rose in strident yells that wasn't quite covered by the loud music crashing from the big room.

"Callan?" Eryn took a deep breath to steady her nerves. "Are you ready?"

"Yeah. Just get clear, Eryn. This is what I do. I don't want you hurt."

"I don't want you hurt, either." Eryn crossed to the emergency door and took out the battery-powered screwdriver she'd borrowed from Callan's kit. The panic bar had hex screws instead of Phillips. She switched out the bit and started unscrewing the alarm cover. She barely managed to keep her hands from shaking so much she couldn't do the job. The loosened screws spilled through her fingers to the floor and she let them go.

Less than a minute after she started, she was inside the alarm system. It was just like several of the others she had helped install during her repo days. The recovery agent had moonlighted installing security systems, and she had learned a lot.

She shoved the screwdriver in, popped the battery backup out, then cut the power supply line. With the alarm system disconnected, she leaned a hip into the panic bar and opened the door.

Callan stood outside in the bright morning sunlight. His jacket lay at his feet. The guns at his hip and under his left arm looked wicked and dangerous. He held a cut-down pump-action shotgun in his hands. His face was hard and implacable, and the aviators covered his eyes. He wore a Kevlar vest. Despite all that, she knew he was vulnerable.

"Get clear. Now." Callan strode into the hallway and headed for the office door.

As she watched him, Eryn's heart trip-hammered and blood rushed through her head. Fear that she was going to lose him in the next few minutes rattled through her no matter how hard she struggled to put them off.

Before Callan reached the office, the door opened and one of the kidnappers stepped out, dragging Toby by the handcuffs the man now wore. The hulking man took in Callan at a glance, released his hold on the cuff chain and reached for the large revolver at his hip.

"He's here!"

Released, Toby dropped to the floor. Blood stained his face. Whatever had gone wrong inside the room had quickly turned violent. He saw Callan and cowered.

Callan raised the shotgun to his shoulder as the kidnapper's gun cleared leather. "Drop it!"

The kidnapper kept bringing his pistol up. Callan fired and the shotgun blast hit the man in the chest and drove him back into the office. He tripped over Toby and sprawled loosely onto the floor. The bloody mess on his shirtfront offered mute testimony that he wasn't getting up again.

Eryn saw at least three men inside the office. One of them was Dylan Mott. She recognized the other two from the pictures they'd found of Mott and his crew.

All of them pulled out weapons and in the next instant bullets raked grooves and chewed holes in the hallway walls and ceiling. Eryn dropped down to a kneeling position and took a two-handed grip on her pistol.

Callan never broke stride as he walked toward the office and fired round after round into the room. Wooden bookshelves on the wall behind the desk exploded in a rush of splinters and spilled a haphazard stack of receipt books and journals to the floor. More buckshot punched holes through the desk.

One of the men hid behind the door and shot around it. Callan adjusted his aim and fired again. The tight spray of buckshot tore through the wooden door and slapped the kidnapper backward. Another shotgun blast struck the man again as he fell. His body draped over Toby's legs.

Still moving, Callan dropped the shotgun and drew one of the pistols. He went forward, totally merciless. Looking at Callan, Eryn had a hard time remembering this was the man who had talked gently to and about his sister. The man who had made love to her just a short time ago. At the moment, there seemed to be nothing left of that man, and the ease that he could so efficiently erase that softer side scared her.

One of those two sides, warrior and lover, had to be more true than the other, and she didn't know which it was.

Another gun went off behind Eryn. Surprised, she realized that she hadn't been watching Callan's back. The kidnapper who had been sitting in the entertainment area had come around the corner and had opened fire. He stood in a wide-legged stance with his pistol up in front of him.

There was no hesitation inside Eryn as she swiveled around and brought her pistol up. She aimed instinctively for the man's center mass, just as she'd been trained, and she fired immediately.

The man staggered and went down with a surprised look.

Pushing herself up, Eryn stayed low as she went back to the man. He was motionless, eyes closed and she didn't know if he was alive or dead. Panic and guilt thrummed inside her, but she worked past it and focused on her need to survive, her need to protect Callan. Gunfire still crashed behind her. She took the man's weapon.

Beyond the corner of the hallway, the few patrons were beating hasty retreats with a skill that showed experience. No one else was coming toward the hallway.

Eryn retreated toward the office. Callan had stepped inside and the fusillade of shots died away. Her heart was in her throat till she eased past the door and spotted Callan peering through a shattered window. He was inserting a fresh magazine into one of his pistols.

The bodies of three other men lay on the floor. None of them was Dylan Mott.

Eryn met Callan's gaze. "Mott?"

"Still on the loose. But not for long."

Glancing around the room, Eryn saw that someone else was also conspicuously absent. "Where's Daniel?"

Callan shook his head. "Not here."

The statement hammered Eryn. If Daniel Steadman wasn't in the office, where was he?

Callan moved back to Toby, but he was talking to Koenig. "Do you have eyes on Mott?"

"I do. I temporarily own the eyes of this city."

Stopping at Toby's side, Callan surveyed the man.

Toby lay on his back with a fearful expression. "Callan. I'm glad to see you. These guys were going to kill me."

Callan pointed his pistol at Toby's face. The man tried to draw back and sink into the floor, but it wasn't working for him. "Where's Daniel?"

Toby shook his head. He mewled in fear. "I don't know. I swear. I don't know. I didn't have anything to do with this."

"Watch him." Eryn holstered her weapon and knelt down to go through Toby's pockets. Honestly, she believed he was innocent. He was too simple to get involved in the kidnapping. But he knew something that he wasn't telling them. She was certain about that.

She took out his wallet and his cell. She pulled up the recent calls and found they were all to the same person: Sierra. Eryn remembered that Sierra was Toby's sister. She touched the information control and the window filled with Sierra's statistics.

The most telling thing was the picture. Sierra Ballard was a beautiful young woman. She had striking red hair that Eryn found memorable. She held the phone up to Callan, displaying the picture of Sierra Ballard.

"Callan."

He made the connection at once. "Your sister is behind this."

Toby spoke quickly, frantically. "Sierra was never able to get over the way Daniel dropped her for Jenny. From the time she was little, Sierra always said she was going to marry Daniel." He shook his head. "I didn't know she was involved. I didn't think she'd do something like this. This is crazy. I didn't have a clue." He swallowed and his heart pumped at his throat. "Not until you told me about the keycard. Sierra could have borrowed it and I wouldn't have known." He closed his eyes and lay back.

Koenig broke in. "Dude, we've got a problem."

Callan relaxed a little and pulled the pistol out of Toby's face. "Yeah?"

"The timetable on the ransom delivery has been changed. The call just went through to the Steadman's number."

"When is the ransom drop?"

"Now."

Eryn tried to process that. "I thought the Steadmans were waiting on the money."

"It's after nine, dude. Banks have been open for a while. Steadman the father pulled out all the stops and got everything lined up. They've got the money ready to transfer."

Eryn's hopes rose for just a moment, then she remembered what Toby had said about his sister. Sierra wanted Daniel. She'd persuaded Dylan Mott to take part in the kidnapping, probably by dangling a big payday in front of him.

She looked at Callan. "Sierra won't kill Daniel. Not if what Toby says is true."

Callan shook his head. "Sierra's not calling all the shots. She never was. Mott's not going to leave a lot of witnesses behind. He's going to clean house before he pulls his vanishing act." He stepped over Toby and headed back into the hallway.

Eryn followed.

Chapter 21

In the hallway, Callan picked up the shotgun, holstered his pistol and started reloading the twelve-gauge. He pushed through the side door and picked up his jacket before heading for the Challenger parked only a short distance away. His blood throbbed in his veins. He didn't have to look over his shoulder to see if Eryn was still there. Her footsteps pounded after him.

"Koenig, do you still have Mott?"

"I do. He can't escape me now. I am righteous wrath and I will be on him as long as you need me to. He's headed toward the Strip. But we've got another problem, dude."

"What?"

"I tapped Jenny's phone to keep an eye on her. She's one of the variables in this mess. Standard operating procedure. Nothing personal."

Koenig was wrong about that. This was all personal. Callan pressed the electronic release on the locks, opened the door, and halted. He looked at Eryn and tossed her the keys. "You drive. It's your city."

She caught the keys in midair and slipped in behind the wheel as he raced around the car.

"What about Jenny?" Callan slipped the seat belt into place as Eryn put the car in Reverse, burned rubber backing up and shot out of the parking lot in a tire-eating shriek.

"She's in play."

"She's not at the hotel anymore?"

"No, dude. She left. Just now. She's in a car."

"Why?"

"Girl detective, can you hear me?"

Eryn pulled to a stop at the light. "Yes."

"I'm downloading a tag onto the car's GPS. The triangle shape is Mott."

"You can do that?"

"GPS system in that car has special modifications, and I am who I am."

Eryn took the next left and sped up. The acceleration pushed Callan back into the seat, but he hardly noticed. His mind was on Jenny and the fact that she was probably headed into danger. There was only one reason she would leave that hotel, and that was to go to Daniel.

"Toby's sister got to her, dude. I just heard the conversation between them because I've been busy watching over you. She told Jenny that she knew where Daniel was, and that she needed to come with her if she wanted to see him alive again."

A huge knot formed in Callan's gut. He gripped the shotgun hard and worked to keep calm. "This wasn't about Daniel, Koenig. This was about my sister. Sierra is going to kill her and stage it to look like she rescued Daniel. She might be in the kidnapping for part of the money, but she's definitely in it for revenge against Jenny."

"That's the way I read it, too."

Eryn reached across and put her hand on Callan's arm. She squeezed gently. "It's okay. We can do this. She's going to be fine."

Callan closed his eyes and took a deep breath. He cleared his mind of the pain and doubt. Eryn provided an unexpected anchor and he took strength from her presence. Then he opened his eyes and focused on the streets.

"Take me to them."

* * *

Eryn didn't know if Callan's growled order was for her or Koenig. She started to draw her hand away, but Callan dropped his hand over hers briefly and looked into her eyes. "Thank you."

"No prob. It's going to be okay, Callan. They can't beat us." She smiled at him and hoped she wasn't lying through her teeth. Then she concentrated on her driving, speeding up more and hoping that a patrol car didn't fall in behind them to try to pull them over.

She followed Mott's triangle down the Strip and across it, whipping by the Tropicana, Excalibur, MGM Grand, Planet Hollywood, Flamingo, the Mirage, Circus Circus and took a hard right onto Fremont Street that sent pedestrians crossing at the light sprinting for cover. They were headed toward the Fremont East District. A parade of bars and clubs lined the area.

There were enough small businesses in the area that someone wanting to get lost could do exactly that.

"Okay, people, you should be within sighting distance. Mott is in a bright yellow Camaro. Guy doesn't go in for stealth. He's stopped a quarter mile ahead of your position." Koenig's voice was calm, steady.

"What kind of car is my sister in?"

"Black Lexus sportback, and it's registered to Sierra Ballard. That car should also be visible."

Eryn scanned the street ahead while dodging through traffic. She spotted the Camaro at the same time Callan did. In the next moment, the Lexus pulled in beside the Camaro.

"Can you throw this car into a controlled slide?" Callan's attention was riveted on the Camaro.

"I think so."

"Bring it around in a one-eighty, so that my side of the car is facing Mott. I'm going to get out. You stay with the car in case someone gets the chance to make a run for it."

"You're going to be in the open."

"So is Mott." Callan looked at her with those slate-gray eyes behind the aviators. "We don't have time. They have the edge. This is all we have."

Torn, Eryn nodded. Just as she was about to pass the Camaro, she cut across traffic, stomped the brakes to tear the tires free of the street, then pulled hard on the wheel and feathered the accelerator to keep the car spinning. She'd learned the procedure in a defensive driving class she'd taken while getting her security license.

The car's speed diminished greatly, but she still couldn't believe it when Callan stepped out of the car and strode toward the Camaro. The car finally came to a stop and she slid the transmission into Park. She opened her door and stepped out, but followed Callan's instructions to stay with the vehicle.

Gripping her pistol in both hands, she stared in amazement as Callan strode like an Old West gunman across the thirty feet separating him from Dylan Mott and one other surviving member of the kidnapping team.

Shots rang out and Callan staggered, once, twice, but he started firing, too. Dylan Mott stood outside the Camaro, using it as a shield. That didn't last long. One of the shotgun blasts caught him in the face and he jerked back and fell. Callan's next shot struck the other gunner in the chest and put him down as well.

By that time, Sierra Ballard had hauled Jenny out of the car and held her in front of her as a shield. A small pistol gleamed in her fist. She yelled in a near-hysterical voice. "Stay back! Stay back or I'm going to kill her!"

Calmly, as if he had all day, Callan racked the shotgun's slide, changed hands with it and dropped the weapon to one side. He drew one of the pistols. He never broke stride. He never said a word.

To Eryn, Callan resembled an Old World avenger, emotionless and lethal. He didn't look anything like the man she'd made love to only that morning. Watching him, watching the cold-blooded way he went about his business even with his sister's life on the line, Eryn was afraid she'd never see that soft part of him again.

Especially not if something happened to Jenny.

Eryn kept her pistol trained on Sierra. If the woman fired, at either of the targets in front of her, Eryn knew she was going to kill Sierra.

Callan kept walking. His gaze never wavered from Sierra. Eryn was surprised that Callan hadn't already shot the woman, then she realized that Callan was afraid that even dying the woman would manage to get off a shot.

Five feet away, Sierra's nerve broke. With a horrifying screech of frustration, she yanked the pistol from Jenny's head and pointed it at Callan. She snapped off two shots in quick succession before Callan dropped her with a single bullet.

He stood there swaying, looking at his sister, guns in both his hands. After a moment, she ran to him. Callan dropped the shotgun to the street and wrapped his arm around her. He held on to her.

Eryn's throat hurt and there were tears in her eyes. Then something thumped in the Camaro's trunk. Eryn walked over and reached inside the sports car to open the trunk.

When the lid lifted, Eryn gazed down to find Daniel Steadman, bloodied and bruised, lying in the trunk. His hands were cuffed behind his back and a gag was in his mouth.

Using her picks, Eryn unlocked the cuffs then removed the gag from his mouth. By that time Jenny had seen him and had run over to be with him.

Excited and scared and feeling some kind of wonderful she'd never felt before, Eryn looked over at Callan. He stood there unsteadily, bleeding from at least three wounds, his left shoulder, his right thigh, and just above his collarbone where the vest hadn't covered. He started to nod, then he faltered and dropped to one knee.

Eryn ran to him. "Callan!" She wrapped her arms around him, lending him her strength. "Callan!"

He looked up at her and smiled. "You did good."

Eryn tore at his shirt. "You're bleeding."

"It's okay. Just give me a minute to catch my breath."

"Your breath! You could be dying."

He shook his head. "I'm not gonna die. I've been shot before. This isn't going to kill me."

"It had better not. You had better not die. You had better not leave me."

Callan cupped his hand behind her head as she knelt with him. "I'm not going to leave you, Eryn. I just found you." He reached around her and held her fiercely. Feeling the strength in him, that undeniable determination to live, Eryn knew it was true. She clung to that as the neighborhood filled up with screaming sirens.

Epilogue

Three days later, after Callan was released from the hospital and most of the legal problems had been resolved, Eryn sat in the audience of Mr. and Mrs. Daniel Steadman's wedding. The best man looked a little battered and worn in his sling and the bandages on his face, but Eryn thought he was the handsomest man in the room.

Later, at the reception, Eryn stood with Callan at the back of the room. He looked slightly gray, but he was holding up.

"Are you sure you don't need to go back to the hotel?"

Callan shook his head. "This is my sister's wedding. I've missed a lot of other things in her life, but I'm not going to miss this."

"They're going to honeymoon in Vegas for a week before they take off to Hawaii. You could visit later."

"No." Callan looked at her and ran his free hand through her hair. "I'm glad you came."

"Hey, I helped save the groom, right? I deserve cake."

Callan laughed. "You deserve a lot more than that."

"And you'd better believe I'm going to get it, mister. One day at a time."

For a moment they stood there in comfortable silence. Jenny and Daniel were a beautiful bride and groom and they deserved the limelight.

"I hear all the legal charges have been dropped."

Callan nodded. "Evidently the Steadman lawyers are very good at what they do. And it helped that they found evidence of blackmail, drugs and other criminal activities at the Invincible offices. The cops weren't quite so eager to prosecute. I also hear you still have a job at CyberStealth."

Eryn smiled and nodded. That had been especially satisfying. Seeing the look on Arthur Briggs's face while the media had been touting her as a real, live private eye hero had been immensely entertaining.

"Not only do I still have my job there, partly because of the Steadman family's interest in buying shares in CyberStealth, but I was promised a raise."

"Congratulations."

"But I don't think I'm going to take it."

Callan raised an eyebrow.

"I've heard a lot about Texas, but I've never been there."

"It's a big state."

"That's one of the things I heard. I've been talking to Mr. Steadman, after he graciously thanked me for saving his son's life."

"You did that."

"He pointed out that family is important, and I tend to agree. He suggested I might want to relocate to Texas and go into business for myself. He guaranteed me plenty of work."

"Generous man."

"He says there will be a lot of work. Not only does he have children, but he plans on having grandchildren as well."

"And he's ambitious."

Eryn smiled at Callan. "I've also been talking to Jenny. She and Daniel plan to start a family quickly, so the demands of personal protection for the Steadman brood is already multiplying."

"I guess so."

"Jenny told me she wants to be a mom, the best mom she can be. But the only way she feels she can do that is to have the best uncle in the world. I graciously pointed out that you were all they had, but maybe you would pass muster."

Callan hesitated at that. "I haven't been around families in a long time."

"Then maybe it's time you started." Eryn put her arms around his waist and held him tight. "I'm actually thinking about taking on a partner at my new security business. Interested?"

Callan gazed at his sister, who was busy chatting with her friends and adoring her new husband. Then he turned his attention back to Eryn. "Yeah. Yeah, I am." And he leaned down and branded her with a kiss.

* * * * *

Harlequin

ROMANTIC
SUSPENSE

COMING NEXT MONTH

Available August 30, 2011

You can find more information on upcoming
Harlequin® titles, free excerpts and more at
www.HarlequinInsideRomance.com.

REQUEST YOUR FREE BOOKS!
2 FREE NOVELS PLUS 2 FREE GIFTS!

ROMANTIC
SUSPENSE

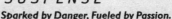

Sparked by Danger, Fueled by Passion.

YES! Please send me 2 FREE Harlequin® Romantic Suspense novels and my 2 FREE gifts (gifts are worth about $10). After receiving them, if I don't wish to receive any more books, I can return the shipping statement marked "cancel." If I don't cancel, I will receive 4 brand-new novels every month and be billed just $4.49 per book in the U.S. or $5.24 per book in Canada. That's a saving of at least 14% off the cover price! It's quite a bargain! Shipping and handling is just 50¢ per book in the U.S. and 75¢ per book in Canada.* I understand that accepting the 2 free books and gifts places me under no obligation to buy anything. I can always return a shipment and cancel at any time. Even if I never buy another book, the two free books and gifts are mine to keep forever.

240/340 HDN FEFR

Name _____ (PLEASE PRINT)

Address _____ Apt. #

City _____ State/Prov. _____ Zip/Postal Code

Signature (if under 18, a parent or guardian must sign)

Mail to the Reader Service:
IN U.S.A.: P.O. Box 1867, Buffalo, NY 14240-1867
IN CANADA: P.O. Box 609, Fort Erie, Ontario L2A 5X3

Not valid for current subscribers to Harlequin Romantic Suspense books.

Want to try two free books from another line?
Call 1-800-873-8635 or visit www.ReaderService.com.

* Terms and prices subject to change without notice. Prices do not include applicable taxes. Sales tax applicable in N.Y. Canadian residents will be charged applicable taxes. Offer not valid in Quebec. This offer is limited to one order per household. All orders subject to credit approval. Credit or debit balances in a customer's account(s) may be offset by any other outstanding balance owed by or to the customer. Please allow 4 to 6 weeks for delivery. Offer available while quantities last.

Your Privacy—The Reader Service is committed to protecting your privacy. Our Privacy Policy is available online at www.ReaderService.com or upon request from the Reader Service.

We make a portion of our mailing list available to reputable third parties that offer products we believe may interest you. If you prefer that we not exchange your name with third parties, or if you wish to clarify or modify your communication preferences, please visit us at www.ReaderService.com/consumerschoice or write to us at Reader Service Preference Service, P.O. Box 9062, Buffalo, NY 14269. Include your complete name and address.

HRS11B